ELFHOME

SUMMONED TO ANOTHER WORLD AND FORCED TO FIGHT THE DEMON KING

BOOK FIVE

JAMES E. WISHER

SAND HILL PUBLISHING

CHAPTER 1

The Western Trade Road, snow covered and endless, stretched out before Danny as he rushed onward, his legs pumping with magically enhanced speed. Skeletal trees flashed by in a blur of white and gray. There were no markers to indicate where the road ended and the surrounding trees began, but the tufts of grass jutting up through the snow let him know he was still on track.

He'd been running for two weeks, stopping only briefly to rest and eat, leaving Discourt far behind. A few villages had come and gone, but Danny ignored them and kept running. With his luck, if he stopped, he'd be certain to find trouble. While he was curious to learn whether or not the plague had spread this far yet, he wasn't that curious. Elfhome couldn't be more than a week away and he wanted to get there as soon as possible.

Noon was fast approaching when shouts pierced the stillness, halting him midstride. It was the first sound he'd heard in days aside from the pounding of his feet and it jarred him.

He cocked his head, listening, as he reached out with the ether. Off to one side of the road, he sensed a dozen life forces. Mostly human, but one nonhuman. Danny had spent enough time around the beastfolk that he was pretty sure the final life force was one of them.

The thuds and yelps continued in a steady rhythm of pain. Danny's jaw clenched. Whatever was going on, it was none of his business. He should just keep moving, but...

But he couldn't walk away if someone was in trouble. Stupid, but it was who he was. Cursing himself all the way, he turned off the road toward the commotion.

He spotted the group at the base of a little hill. Eleven men surrounded a fallen figure, kicking and jeering as they beat the shit out of him. The crumpled beastfolk—the thick hair on his arms and legs confirmed the victim's identity— curled into a ball and tried to shield his head with his arms.

Danny hated few things more than he hated bullies. "Hey!"

The men whirled around, their victim forgotten for the moment. Danny closed the distance in seconds and crossed his arms. They weren't warriors, that was clear at a glance. The men wore no armor and only carried modest daggers on their belts. They were likely farmers or shepherds from a nearby village.

"You think eleven's enough of you to beat up one person? Takes a lot of guts with those odds."

"Stinking beastman came begging at our village," one of the men said. "Everyone knows their kind carry the plague. We figured we'd make it clear he wasn't welcome around here. Or anywhere else for that matter."

Danny stared at the man. He couldn't be that stupid. Then again, given what they were doing, maybe he could.

"Let me get this straight," he said. "You think this beastman is a plague carrier, and, having come to this conclusion, you thought surrounding him and making physical contact would be a good idea?"

"I... Well, no. We wanted to make sure he didn't come back." A lot of the man's anger had been replaced by trepidation as he realized what they were doing.

"And if you're right, you're likely all infected, and when you return home, you'll end up killing your whole village. Brilliant."

"What else could we have done?" The fear and desperation in his voice made Danny sigh.

"Spoke to him from a distance and asked him to move on? Does your village not have a priest who could tell if he was sick?"

"No, Father Alex died three months ago. Not from the plague!" the man hastened to add. "He was about ninety. The temple hasn't assigned anyone else to our village yet."

Danny nodded. That certainly explained their anxiety. "I understand your fear, truly, I do, but you can't use it to justify this sort of behavior. I'm an arcane knight and I can confirm that he isn't sick and neither are any of you. Go home, protect your families, but don't let your fear turn you into monsters. We have enough of those already."

"He really isn't sick?" the spokesman asked.

"No, he really isn't. You nearly beat a harmless man to death."

They hung their heads and muttered amongst themselves. Danny said nothing, content to let them work it out for themselves as long as they didn't start kicking the beastman again.

At last the men turned and trudged off without so much

as a word to him or an apology to their victim. Not what he would've preferred, but at least they weren't still beating the poor guy.

Danny watched until they disappeared from view before crouching beside the beastman. "Hang on, I'll get you sorted out."

He sent holy energy into the beastman, accelerating his healing until the many cuts and bruises faded away. "Better?"

The beastman rolled over on his back and stared up at Danny. "Why help me and not your fellow humans? I hate your kind and you clearly hate mine."

He sounded young. At first Danny thought he was an adult, but his voice combined with a relatively slight build made it clear he was an adolescent.

"If I hated your kind, I wouldn't have bothered healing you. I've met plenty of beastfolk and gotten along with all of them. Don't let the bad actions of a few sour you on the whole species, that'll make you just as bad as the idiots who hate beastfolk for being beastfolk and not humans."

The youth sat up. "Who did you meet?" He sounded eager rather than sullen now.

"I'm on good terms with Rafe's pack and I met another pack leader named Val, though he—"

"You met Val! Where is he? Is he okay?"

"He was fine when we parted company." Danny gave him a brief rundown of his rescue of Val and the other beastfolk slaves. "They should be safe in that elf outpost for as long as they care to stay. How do you know Val?"

"He's my pack leader. When they separated us, I feared he was being taken to execution." The youth finally looked Danny in the eye. "My name is Briggs. Thank you for saving them."

Danny stood and held out his hand. "Ronin, and it was my pleasure. I told Val I'd keep an eye out for the still-missing beastfolk, but I haven't had much luck finding them. You're the first I've met since parting company with him."

Briggs took his hand and Danny pulled him to his feet. His leather vest was torn and his trousers weren't in much better shape. If he'd had a cloak at some point, he'd lost it. Briggs looked like a beggar and smelled almost as bad.

"I know where they are, more or less, but I'm too weak to save them. That's why I'm going to the elf forest. Legends say the demons will give you power in exchange for your soul. I'll do anything for the strength to save my pack."

"As it happens, I'm on my way to the forest as well. Perhaps it would be wise for us to travel together. We can share stories."

"I would like that, Ronin. I've been wandering, struggling to survive as I worked my way west after escaping the slavers. Every pack between here and the forest has been taken and the humans wouldn't let me approach their villages, though this is the first where I was attacked."

"The slavers didn't send anyone after you?" Danny opened his satchel and offered Briggs a strip of jerky. The young man stuffed it in his mouth whole, half chewed it, and nearly choked as he swallowed.

"They had over a hundred prisoners from ten packs. I doubt I was worth the effort. One youth, on his own, at this time of year? They no doubt assumed I'd be dead before long. But I survived." Briggs shot him a fierce look. "And I'll make them pay for what they did to my pack."

Danny couldn't fault his determination, though the whole "trading your soul for power" thing didn't sound like the best idea. But it was Briggs's choice, not Danny's.

He held out a second strip of jerky. "More?"

"Thank you." Briggs took the second strip and ate it at a more reasonable pace.

Danny set out for the trade road, a piece of jerky in his own mouth. It seemed he'd acquired another traveling companion. Much like Lise, Briggs would slow him down, but if he got information about the missing beastfolk, it would be worth it. Plus, Danny kind of liked the kid's spunk. You had to respect that sort of dedication.

He decided if there was some way he could help Briggs, he would. It would also let him keep his promise to Val which made a nice bonus.

⟳

The biting wind cut through Danny's heavy cloak as he led Briggs off the trade road toward a small clearing nestled at the base of a low hill. It looked like a good spot to set up camp for the night. Hopefully the hill would protect them from the worst of the wind. Danny blew out a white breath when they passed behind the hill and it did indeed cut the wind down to little more than an annoyance.

He glanced at his companion. Briggs appeared unfazed by the cold despite his lack of a cloak. It seemed beastfolk weren't only immune to illness, they were also tougher than humans. Must be nice.

A frozen-over stream ran not far from his chosen campsite. Though he hadn't planned it, Danny wouldn't complain about a convenient source of water.

A wave of his hand blasted the snow away, giving them a

clear space to make camp. Danny only had his one-person tent which he pulled out of storage and started to set up.

"Will you be okay sleeping outside?" Danny asked.

"Of course, I've been doing so since I escaped." Briggs thrust out his thin chest. "We beastfolk are a tough lot. It'll take more than a little cold to get the best of me."

Danny smiled at his bravado and ignored the faint shiver shaking Briggs from head to toe. He gathered an armful of firewood from storage and set about building a small campfire. Once that was going, Danny put some sausages on to sizzle. The way Briggs hovered behind him, sniffing loudly at the scent of the food made it clear he was more interested in eating than the warmth of the fire.

"The sausage will take a little while to cook through," Danny said. "Why don't you tell me what happened to your pack?"

Briggs blew out a long sigh. "There's not much to tell. We were asleep in camp. I don't know what time, but late at night. Human soldiers came rushing in, burning tents and beating unconscious anyone who didn't immediately surrender. It happened so fast. I tried to protect my mother, but someone hit me on the side of the head. When I woke, I was chained up along with everyone else."

That meshed with what Val had told him and what he saw firsthand in Rafe's camp. "What happened next?"

Briggs's youthful face twisted into a snarl. "They separated us. Val and two other hunters were taken away. The rest of us they marched north. After four days they grew overconfident. Mom helped me escape my shackles. I didn't want to leave her, but she said if no one escaped, there would be no hope of rescue."

He paused, hands clenched into fists. Danny turned the sausages. Stories like this couldn't be rushed.

At last Briggs said, "So I ran away. I left the others behind and flew like a coward. I didn't have a plan other than putting as much distance between me and the soldiers as possible. Eventually I remembered the stories our shaman used to tell about the demon forest. She said it as a warning, but I saw hope. With the power of a demon, I'll find my mother and the rest of our pack and save them."

Danny nodded. The kid had guts, no question. Making a deal with a demon wasn't the wisest strategy, but Danny wasn't foolish enough to imagine Briggs would listen to him. He was too angry and filled with thoughts of revenge. Maybe that would change in time. Hopefully not before he did something he couldn't undo.

When the sausages were nice and crispy on the outside. Danny speared one on a fork and handed it to Briggs then took a second for himself. They were the spicy ones he'd gotten a taste for in Discourt. Hopefully they wouldn't be too much for Briggs.

The kid showed no signs of discomfort and soon the food was gone. "Very good. I've never eaten food like that. Is all human food so full of flavor?"

Danny grinned. A fellow chili head, cool. "Not all of it, but the best of it is. Have you ever had bacon?"

Briggs shook his head. "Is it good?"

"My young friend, you are in for a revelation at breakfast." Danny swallowed a sigh. "But for now I suppose I should tell my part of the story."

Danny laid out everything he'd learned as it related to the beastfolk. "I'm optimistic that there won't be any more kidnappings, now that I've dealt with the leaders of the group. I fear freeing those taken will be more difficult. From what I've heard, the northerners are well known for their embrace of raiding and slave taking. I can't go to war with an entire people."

"I wouldn't ask you to," Briggs said. "You've already done more for my people than any other human ever has. This battle is for beastfolk to fight. Any help you can offer would be welcome, but we won't ask you to fight our battles for us. If you can help me reach the demon forest then show me where Val and the others are, that will be enough."

"I can do that, no problem. In fact, we should reach the forest in another week to ten days."

Briggs flashed a predatory grin. "Then I get my power and those who hurt my family will suffer."

Danny hoped it worked out the way he wanted, but when demons were involved, nothing went as you'd expect.

CHAPTER 2

The towering trees of Elfhome loomed ahead. Danny had visited a redwood forest on Earth and those trees couldn't hold a candle to these. They had to be at least twice as big as that tree you could drive your car through.

He and Briggs had left the Western Trade Road behind a couple of days ago when they first spotted the trees in the distance. Now that they were only a few miles away, Danny could sense the forest's corruption. Any doubts he'd had about the presence of demons was long gone.

"I don't like the look of this," Briggs said. "I got a chill and not from the cold."

"It's the corruption," Danny said. "Non-wizards experience it in different ways. Some feel a chill, others feel nauseous, and many just want to run away. The last group are the smart ones. You can't hurt a demon without magic or mithril."

"I came here to make a deal, not to fight."

Danny's smile held no humor. "What you want and what

the demons want aren't necessarily the same thing. A lot of them are too stupid to think about making a deal, they only know how to rend and tear."

"That's not very encouraging."

Danny shrugged. "I wasn't trying to be encouraging. This is your last chance to turn back."

Briggs straightened and looked him in the eye. "I'm not turning back."

"Okay."

With each step the sense of corruption grew stronger. It was different from Fell Forest, more focused, like the source was in the center and from there it radiated out in waves. Which made sense if the city was hidden in the middle of the forest.

A few strides from the first tree Danny drew his sword. "Stay close."

"Don't worry," Briggs said. "I plan to."

The dirt road they'd been following gradually narrowed, dwindling to a rough path strewn with roots and vines that twisted underfoot like serpents. The trees closed in around them, blotting out the sun and making the cold even worse.

Danny glanced at one of the massive evergreens as they passed. Despite the corruption emanating from the woods, the trees themselves appeared unchanged. There were even chirping birds in the canopy. A few yards deeper in the skittering of some small animal caught his attention. This was definitely different from Fell Forest, more controlled. Weird for a place run by demons.

The shadows thickened around them as they ventured further into the forest. The deep grooves of the bark reminded him of a giant's knuckles. Not a pleasant memory. Danny's eyes darted from side to side. It felt like everything was a threat, but he couldn't let the feeling overwhelm him. His instincts screamed that the moment he did, it would be the end of him.

As if summoned by the thought, a dark shape leapt out from behind one of the trunks, lunging toward them with terrifying speed.

Danny reacted before he could think, his sword flashing out in a deadly arc, its blade charged with holy energy.

The demon died silently as the blade sliced through its torso.

As it slowly started to dissolve into the familiar black goo, Danny gave it a closer look. The demon had black skin like polished obsidian. Its features were poorly formed; a vague protrusion served as a nose and two depressions above that as eyes. It had no mouth or ears. It was screwed up in a completely different way from the other demons he'd encountered during his time on this world.

"Is that a demon?" Briggs asked. "I've never seen one before."

"Consider yourself lucky. The vast majority of people who see them never see anything else. Come on."

They pressed on, the corruption growing thicker and more oppressive with each step. The attacks came at irregular intervals. The demons, all of them identical to the first one he killed, grew stronger and more numerous with each attack. But never so strong that Danny felt pushed to the brink. He hadn't even needed to use the ethersword.

It was weird, but he wasn't about to complain about the enemies being too weak.

Fifty paces from the site of his most recent battle, the forest started to thin before giving way to a sight that stole Danny's breath. Gleaming steel towers like miniature skyscrapers filled a huge clearing. This had to be the elf-blood capital.

A shadow passed over them before a figure of dark beauty descended from the sky. The female demon was stunning. She landed in front of them, her black raven wings folding behind her. What he could only call a black ninja costume hugged her curves like a second skin and a sword hilt jutted up beside her right ear. Her perfect, heart-shaped face was pale and her eyes glowed red.

This had to be the demon Avius mentioned. Based on her looks, he feared she might be a servant of Ardent Lilly.

Danny readied his sword. He had no doubt this would be a far harder battle than any he'd fought so far.

"Welcome to Elfhome, Daniel J. Smith," she said. "The master is eager to speak with you."

Of all the possibilities Danny had considered, a polite welcome hadn't made the list.

"I thought you said your name was Ronin," Briggs said, snapping Danny out of his stupor.

"Ronin is my adventurer name. Daniel was the name my parents gave me." He shot the demon a hard look. "How do you know it?"

"The master told me. You came here from his Earth, so of course he knows your name."

"You serve the Reaper."

"Yes. My name is Riko and I have the honor of serving as one of his black-winged angels."

"How did the Reaper know I'd come here?" Danny asked.

"He's been watching you since the moment you were taken from his Earth. The master dislikes few things more than when someone steals from him. While I was told to expect you, I wasn't told to expect him. Who is your companion?"

Danny took a breath to introduce Briggs, but before he could speak, Briggs stepped up and did it himself. "My name is Briggs and I've come to pledge my soul for the power to save my pack. I was told the demons of this forest had the power to grant my wish."

Riko looked from Briggs to Danny and back as if uncertain what to think about his request. Finally she said, "I think you may not know what you're asking for, but your determination is strong. Is it your wish that I help him, Daniel?"

Danny shook his head. "Briggs is his own man. Whatever he decides is up to him."

"So be it. As it happens, we have a demonic blade without a wielder at the moment. If young Briggs has the strength and will to master the demon spirit within, it will grant him all the power he can handle. If not..."

"I will accept any risk," Briggs said. "Show me this weapon."

Riko snapped her fingers and a black ball appeared beside her. When it vanished, a two-foot-tall demon that looked a bit like a toad walking on two legs stood waiting. "Take Briggs to Grimshadow's chamber. He wishes to attempt to claim it."

"I will claim it!" Briggs said. "Whatever happens I wanted to thank you, Daniel or Ronin or whatever you want to be called, for everything you've done for me and the beastfolk in general."

"Ronin will do, and it was my pleasure. I've had great respect for your people ever since I met them and you've only added to the good impression. I wish you the best of luck in getting what you want." Danny held out his hand and they shook in the beastfolk way.

Without a backwards look, Briggs followed the toad demon deeper into the city.

Danny put the boy out of his mind and focused on the matter at hand. "I need access to the elf-bloods' library."

"First you must speak with the master. My orders were to bring you to him as soon as you arrived. We've already delayed too long."

The last thing Danny wanted was to speak with a demon lord, but he also knew better than to offend a being that powerful, if only because he might be able to stop Danny from accessing the library.

"I'd love to speak with him. Lead the way."

CHAPTER 3

Riko led Danny deeper into the oddly modern looking city of Elfhome. The tall steel towers blocked off what little light made it through the canopy, making the city feel like it was in permanent twilight. Their footsteps were the only sounds breaking the eerie silence. The corruption was thick enough here that animals weren't willing to approach. Wise of them.

"This place reminds me of an Earth city only the buildings are missing windows. What is it with elf-bloods and not wanting to look outside? I thought they were supposed to be into nature."

"Yes, I remember being surprised when I was summoned here. I never lived in a city, but my duties took me to both Paris and London, so I have seen them. As for the view, elf steel can be made transparent. From the inside you can see out perfectly. It's much more secure than adding glass."

"Wait, you're from Earth?" Danny figured she'd lived on this world when she was alive.

"From your Earth specifically. All the black-winged

angels are. The master has a powerful connection to your world and we, the Daughters of the Reaper, are his most loyal servants. When we die, this is our reward."

Danny wasn't sure if ending up as a demon was much of a reward, but she seemed happy enough.

As cities went, Elfhome wasn't huge. Most of the buildings were roughly the same size and shape, but in the center of the city one tower rose above the rest. The council he read about probably lived there. Danny assumed it would be their destination, but Riko led him to the right where a low, blocky structure radiated the strongest corruption yet. Above the door, an upside-down sword had been bent at a strange angle.

"Did this used to be a temple of Branik?"

"Indeed, the hellpriest who summoned me repurposed it to serve as the master's temple. Not that we have anyone here to offer their prayers."

"Is that a thing demon worshippers do?" Danny asked. "For some reason I always assumed demon worship was more a practical thing than one of faith."

"You're not wrong, but a temple makes it easier for the master to speak with his followers should it be necessary. It serves as a focusing device, for lack of a better description." Riko pressed a rune on the wall and the door dropped out of sight. "Go on in. It's a great honor to speak with the master personally. Despite my years of service, I have only had the honor twice."

Danny wasn't sure how much of an honor it was to speak with a demon lord, but he wasn't about to mock her faith, that would be pointlessly rude.

Steeling himself, he strode into the temple. An ambient red glow left the pews, made of metal, just like everything else, look like they were covered in blood. At the front of the chapel a black stone statue of the Reaper, his scythe clutched in a bony hand, glowered at Danny. The atmosphere was oppressive. It felt like weights had been attached to his ankles. Every stride took all his willpower.

For someone so eager to talk, the Reaper sure didn't make it easy.

One stride from the statue his vision blurred. Reality shifted as darkness swallowed him. When his vision cleared, he found himself standing in a cavernous throne room carved from black stone. More demons like Riko lined the walls. The beautiful women all stared at him with their unsettling red eyes.

And speaking of unsettling, at the far end of the room, on a raised dais, the Reaper himself sat upon a throne of bone. He held his scythe exactly as the statue had.

The empty hood shifted to look at him. "Welcome, Daniel."

That voice, deep, cold, and emotionless, did nothing to make Danny feel welcome. "Thank you, um, sir, for inviting me. What did you want to talk about?"

"You and your mission. Your kidnapping from my Earth and you being used and betrayed by people too stupid to see your true value."

Danny swallowed hard. He knew a recruiting pitch when he heard one. "About my mission. I was hoping to access the elf-blood's library. Will that be a problem?"

"No, you're welcome to read whatever you like. Finding a way to destroy the summoning circle will be no easy task, but if there's a way to do so, you will find it here."

He got permission at least, so far so good. "You're okay with me destroying it?"

"Indeed. I have no wish to see anyone else from my Earth taken away."

Danny frowned. "Is there no way you could've stopped it?"

"No. While I am omnipotent within my hell, beyond it I am forced to act through other, lesser beings. You are the first with both the motivation and the potential power to sever the link. And even then your chances of success are not great." The Reaper shifted on his throne. "Should you choose to pledge your soul to me and become a hellpriest, the additional power you'd gain would improve your chances greatly."

And there was the pitch. It was at least an easy one to answer. "Thank you for the offer, but I'll have to pass. Our philosophies are too different for it to work out."

"I knew you were going to say that. A few words of warning then. I can't be specific for various reasons."

Danny nodded. "The Goddess said something similar. Anything you can tell me would be welcome."

"Aren't you popular. Very well, here are my warnings. One, Ardent Lilly's champion is still alive." Before Danny could point out his disinterest in hunting the demon king down, the Reaper continued. "Some of her hideouts are near sites of power you will need to visit to complete your task. You would do well to be cautious."

That wasn't what Danny expected him to say. "I will be, thank you for the warning. Was there something else?"

"Yes. Adonael will not allow you to take away her advantage without a fight. Expect her followers to do everything they can to stop you."

"When you say everything, I assume you mean they're going to try and kill me."

"Without a doubt." A dark chuckle emerged from the hood. "Heaven can be as merciless as Hell when it's for their precious greater good. Though I cannot aid you directly lest I violate the rules of the game, I can promise that none who serve me will stand in your way. Best of luck."

Danny blinked and found himself back in the temple, his whole body stiff with tension. As meetings went, that one wasn't so bad. Having a demon lord cheering for him felt strange, but it was certainly better than the alternative.

He rolled his shoulders and headed for the door. Riko was waiting for him outside. "How did your conversation go?"

"Well enough, all things considered. He approves of my mission and promised not to do anything to inhibit my success. He also offered to make me a hellpriest, which I turned down."

"Why? It's a great honor."

"Philosophical differences. Could you show me to the library now?"

She favored him with a slightly confused look then shrugged and headed for the large central tower.

Danny had no idea how big the library might be, but he hoped it wouldn't take too long to find what he needed to know.

CHAPTER 4

Briggs tried to keep up a brave front as he walked away from Ronin, but he finally had to look back. His friend was already out of sight, along with the female demon who greeted them. Briggs knew little about demons, but even he could tell how strong she was. Ronin's confidence when dealing with her impressed him as much as anything he'd seen the human do.

"Hey!" the toad demon said. "Keep up. I've got better things to do than search for a lost brat."

Annoying as the demon's attitude was, Briggs was eager for anything to distract him from his racing thoughts. The less time he spent thinking about what he was about to do the better.

"Like what?" Briggs took a few quick strides so he was only a pace behind the demon.

"What?" the demon asked.

"I was curious what you did here. The lady demon seems to be in charge and those black demons were your guards, so I was wondering what you do."

"I'm an imp, I do whatever I'm told. Mostly I wander around and keep an eye on things. Guiding you is the first real task I've had in years. It's been boring, not that anyone cares if an imp is bored. If you could either go stark raving insane or get yourself killed in a spectacularly horrid fashion it would do wonders to relieve my boredom."

"Sorry, Toad, but I have too much to do to die here."

"An imp can hope, can't he?"

Briggs didn't bother to answer and they continued on in silence. Their journey took them away from the city center and down a road with smaller towers which loomed overhead, their perfect steel walls glinting in the dim light.

He'd never visited a place like this and wasn't sure what to make of it. In fact he doubted anyone from his pack had ever visited a place like this. Beastfolk belonged on the plains. Cities were for humans and apparently elf-bloods.

They approached a squat three-story tower and Toad jumped up to tap a spot on the wall. A door dropped out of sight.

"There you go, have fun. I'll be watching from a safe distance. Grimshadow isn't the most pleasant of the master's servants."

Briggs's heart pounded as he stepped inside. His eyes were drawn immediately to the center of the room, where a curved black dagger rested on a stone pedestal. He'd never seen a weapon with that shape before. It was about a foot long and ended in a loop rather than a pommel.

A few strides brought him within touching distance of the weapon. Though he couldn't see it, he felt a pulse of pressure pushing against his chest. Like the dagger had a heartbeat.

Hesitantly he reached out. Six inches from the hilt he

paused. There was no turning back from this, he knew it deep in his soul. This thing, this weapon, was evil. Evil in a way Briggs had never experienced before. He hoped to use it in a good cause, but was it possible to use something so corrupt for good? He didn't know, but what other choice did he have?

The answer was obvious. He had no other options. It was this or letting his pack—his mother—remain in the hands of slavers. And that wasn't happening.

He grasped the hilt and a surge of icy energy shot up his arm, numbing his body. Briggs gasped as a mixture of pain and power filled him.

Briggs cried out as a dark presence slammed into his mind. The world went black and when the darkness cleared he stood face to face with a creature out of his worst nightmares.

The demon, for it could be nothing else, stood on four legs like an Alpha Wolf. Each foot ended in a claw that was an exact match for the dagger. Its body was huge, with rippling muscle, and covered with thick, black fur. A tail that ended in a serpent's head snapped behind it.

"You are weak, boy," the demon said. "Your body will be mine and I will use it to claim lives in the master's name, starting with your human friend."

Briggs clenched his fists and raised them. "I will beat you, demon. I need your power and I will have it."

The demon leapt at him, claws leading.

He dodged and punched it on the flank as it rushed past. A stone would've been softer.

The demon's claws screeched against the stone as it spun back. "You're quick, boy. I give you that. But you can't hurt me."

The demon might be right. Ronin had warned him that only magic and mithril could hurt a demon. Briggs didn't know what mithril was and he had no magic.

Wait. He also had no opponent. This was all in his head. And if it was in his head, he should be able to control it.

The demon crouched, ready to spring again.

Briggs pictured the dagger he was holding in the real world and it appeared in his hand. It felt awkward, but also good. Armed was definitely better than not when facing an opponent.

The demon leapt.

Briggs ducked under its claws and slashed as it passed, opening a long gash in its side. It didn't bleed, thus proving his opponent wasn't real.

"You'll suffer for that, boy."

Briggs said nothing. He lowered his center of balance like his father had taught him and fiddled with his grip on the dagger, trying to find the right way to hold it. He settled on a reverse grip, the curved blade running along his forearm.

The demon roared and rushed in.

It snapped at Briggs, who lashed out with the dagger, driving the tip into the demon's right eye.

It howled in pain.

Briggs had no mercy in him. He would beat this thing no matter what.

The dagger shot out again and again, tearing the beast's face up and putting out its other eye.

An overhead blow drove the dagger down into the demon's skull. It vanished in a flurry of black flames. When the final flame faded away, Briggs found himself back in the tower, the dagger in his hand.

He'd done it.

Even as he reveled in his triumph, Briggs knew this was only the beginning. He had no idea how to use the dagger's magic, and the demon's essence still lingered within. Somehow he doubted this would be the last battle he and the monster fought.

But those battles would come later. For now he was tired and hungry. Hopefully he could join Ronin for dinner. It wasn't only food that interested Briggs. His human friend was a wizard. Surely he could tell him how best to use the dagger's power.

Briggs strode out of the tower and found the toad demon waiting, now far away.

"You're still alive and in possession of your body. Impressive. I figured Grimshadow would gobble you up and take over."

"You might've warned me that was going to happen," Briggs said.

"What fun would that've been? This miserable city is tedious as, well, hell, most of the time. I would never deprive myself of entertainment."

Arguing with Toad was a waste of time. "Can you take me to Ronin?"

The little demon shrugged. "Sure, come on."

Briggs fell in behind him and they marched back toward the city center. He didn't really know if Ronin could help him master the dagger, but even if he couldn't, Briggs would find some other way to make it work. His pack's future depended on it.

CHAPTER 5

Danny followed Riko up the stairs to the central tower's second floor where the elf-bloods' library waited. He had no idea what to expect. Given the odd modernity of the towers, banks of computers wouldn't have been out of place. Of course he hadn't seen anything resembling digital tech, so finding it here was unlikely.

Riko glanced back at him. "You seem nervous. I can feel your emotions from here. Rest assured, no one in the master's service will trouble you. He wishes you to succeed, which means we do as well."

"That's not what has me worried. I've never been much good at bookwork. Couldn't wait to get out of school and swore I'd never go back. This feels like a giant homework assignment."

"The librarian will help you find what you need. There are also bedrooms on the next floor up. Feel free to use any of them you'd like."

"Thanks. To be honest I expected to have to fight my way through an army of demons to reach this place, not just a few weaklings. The warm welcome has been a surprise, though a pleasant one."

"You would've had to if the master didn't expect you. The guardians were just a test to see if you were worthy. Had they killed you, it would've been clear you were unworthy." They reached the second-floor landing and she pushed the door open. "Here we are."

Danny stepped through the arched entryway into the library. His eyes widened as he took in the towering shelves filled with ancient leather-bound tomes that stretched up and disappeared into the shadows of the ceiling high above. The musty scent of aged parchment filled the air.

"Heaven's mercy," he muttered.

The sheer vastness of the space struck him. Row after endless row of bookcases marched off into the distance. There had to be hundreds of thousands of books in here, if not millions. How many of them had information on the summoning ritual? Even a tiny percentage could still be hundreds of books.

He'd be dead of old age before he could read them all.

"Take a breath, Daniel," Riko said. "I can hear your heart racing from here."

Danny nodded, stomping down his rising panic. He'd figure this out one way or another. He owed it to the innocent youths who'd end up dragged here if he failed.

"Right. You mentioned a librarian. Let's hope he's in a helping mood."

"His mood means nothing. Only obeying the master's will matters." Riko lifted a pale hand and snapped her fingers.

From deeper in the library, a stooped figure in dark robes came gliding out from between two shelves, its face hidden in the depths of a hood. The librarian looked like a tiny, incredibly weak version of the Reaper.

The librarian stopped a few feet away, its empty cowl shifting from Riko to Danny and back. "The master's guest, I take it. What information do you require?"

"I'll leave you to your work," Riko said. "If you need anything, just call my name."

"Thanks," Danny said. "I've got plenty of supplies so I should be okay for a while."

She offered a polite bow and withdrew.

Danny turned to the librarian. "I'm looking for information that will allow me to destroy the magic circle connecting my world to this one."

The librarian shifted closer, peering at Danny as if seeing him for the first time. "A project the master has long wished undertaken. And he thinks you capable of completing it? Interesting. You must be stronger than you look. Follow me."

Danny followed the silently gliding figure between towering shelves, his footsteps sounding far too loud as they thunked on the floor. The place was lit by some diffused glow, the source of which Danny couldn't pinpoint. It was pleasant and warm, the sort of light that made reading easier. Most surprising of all, there wasn't a spot of dust to be seen.

"Do you know what all these books contain?" he asked.

"Of course, I wouldn't be much use if I didn't. You're only my third guest in fifteen hundred years."

They turned right, down another row of shelves. "Who were the other two?"

"Hellpriests looking for magical secrets. Unfortunately for them, the elf-bloods had little use for diabolism. Hardly a surprise given the blood of Heaven that ran through their veins. Both hellpriests left disappointed."

"Hopefully my luck will be better."

The librarian didn't respond, which was fine. Danny was mostly talking to break the silence, not because he had anything profound to say.

Finally, the librarian stopped in front of a particular section of shelves and began pulling books down. It handed them one after the next to Danny.

The stack grew heavier with each addition, until he was struggling to keep them all balanced. When he reached ten Danny said, "This is plenty to start with. I can come back for more if I need to."

The librarian paused, another book halfway off the shelf, and turned to face him. "As you wish. Given the average human intellect, it's probably best not to overwhelm yourself."

Danny didn't appreciate the comment, but he couldn't deny the truth of it either. The librarian led him back to the main area of the library and pointed at a table and some chairs off to one side. "Call me if you need anything else."

With that his less-than-charming companion vanished back into the stacks.

"Well, let's see what we've got." Danny set the books down and grabbed the first one from the pile.

He settled in the soft leather chair and opened the cover. The pages crackled when he turned them. The text was written in Elvish, just like the books he took from the Villipan library.

Danny sighed and activated the translation spell. He had no idea how long he'd last but he was determined to finish at least one book before dinner.

CHAPTER 6

D anny shut the leather-bound tome with a weary sigh. How long had he been reading? There was no way to know for sure given the lack of clocks and windows, but considering how stiff he felt, a few hours seemed likely. He yawned and blinked his gritty eyes, trying to work some moisture into them. Prolonged use of the translation spell always left him like this. It was an unfortunate but unavoidable side effect. It wasn't like eye drops were a thing here.

At least he'd made it through the first book in his pile. On the downside, he hadn't gotten much out of it. The whole thing was theory on how the spell worked. It was all about ethereal connections and interplanetary transmission, piercing protective barriers and tunnel theory. All of it soared way over his head while reminding him how smart the elf-blood wizards were.

Lucky for Danny you didn't have to be a genius to smash things.

His stomach grumbled. Right, he hadn't eaten since

morning. He'd had enough of reading for now anyway. Time to find those rooms Riko mentioned and see what he could do about supper. Danny had plenty of supplies in storage, all he needed was somewhere to cook.

Groaning, he hauled himself out of his chair, muscles stiff after reading for so long. He rolled his shoulders and stretched, trying to work out the kinks. A few vertebrae popped, drawing a sigh. He needed to remember to move around more often. The books weren't going anywhere and little breaks might even let him work longer overall.

He grabbed a different book from the pile in case he felt like reading more later and headed for the exit. At the landing, he climbed the steel steps to the third floor. The silence was oppressive. He tried to imagine what this place must've been like at the height of the elf-bloods' empire and failed.

When he reached the third floor, he pressed a glowing rune and the door dropped into the floor. Beyond it waited a long hall running left and right, lined with doors. Having no interest in exploring, Danny went to the nearest door and pressed the rune.

Beyond it he found a simple apartment. There was a modest sitting room with two chairs and a coffee table. Two doorways led to a bedroom and a kitchen. The kitchen had what he assumed was a magic stove of some sort. Hopefully he could figure out how to turn the heat on and start supper. Steak with vegetables might be nice for a change. He had some carrots and parsnips in storage.

Mouth watering, he was about to get started when someone knocked. He frowned. It had to be Riko, no one else knew where to find him, but he couldn't imagine what the demon woman could want.

There was one way to find out. He turned back and

opened the door. Sure enough, Riko was waiting outside along with Briggs. The boy had a wicked-looking karambit clutched in his hand. The blade was black and longer than typical, but that's definitely what it was.

"Your companion asked the imp to guide him to you," Riko said. "I took over."

"I was hungry and I don't have any supplies." Briggs looked a bit sheepish to admit it.

"Not a problem," Danny said. "I was just about to start supper. Come on in. You're welcome to join us as well, Riko."

The demon offered a stunning smile. "I don't require food, but thank you for the invitation. Good evening."

She turned and walked away. With a shrug, Danny shut the door.

Briggs was looking around at the apartment. He seemed okay. Somehow Danny imagined claiming a demon weapon would've taken more of a toll.

He looked closer at the dagger. It fairly oozed corruption. Nasty thing, no doubt.

"Can I see that?" Danny asked.

Briggs jumped when he spoke. Maybe he hadn't come through whatever trial he faced as untouched as it appeared.

"The demon inside is unpleasant. I'm not sure it's a good idea."

"I've dealt with plenty of unpleasant things." Danny held out his hand. "Let me see."

Briggs hesitated but finally handed over the karambit, hilt first. As soon as Danny's fingers closed around the grip, a wave of malevolence washed over him and he was sucked into the darkness. When it cleared he found himself facing a black-furred demon that looked like an Ultra Wolf with a snake tail.

"I know you," the demon growled. "I saw your face in the boy's mind. You were a fool to pick me up, human. I will take over your body and use it to—"

"Yeah, yeah, I've heard it all before. Spare me your pathetic threats." Danny drew ether into his psychic form and grew until he towered over the demon. "Are you sure you want to fight me?"

The demon stared up at him, cowering. "What are you?"

"Just an adventurer. One who's killed demons by the hundreds and who isn't the least impressed with you. Let me make one thing clear. You will not try and take control of Briggs. In fact, you're going to do your best to teach him how to use your powers. If you do otherwise, I'll shred your essence into pieces so small even the Reaper won't be able to put you back together. Do we understand each other?"

"Yes, whatever you say."

Danny smiled and shrank back to his normal size. "That's remarkably reasonable for a demon. I appreciate your attitude."

Despite having four legs, the demon offered a credible shrug. "Demons are immortal. If I can't use this bearer, I'll use the next one. The life of a beastfolk is like the blink of an eye to me. Many lesser demons don't appreciate this, but time is our most powerful asset. As long as we continue to exist, we will always have another chance."

It seemed treating this one as nothing more than a beast would be unwise. Danny made a mental note to be on his guard, not that he ever really lowered it completely.

An effort of will shifted him back to his body and he handed the blade back to Briggs. "You're right, that thing is unpleasant. On the plus side, I think you'll find him a much more reasonable partner now. We'll also have to find you a sheath for that blade at some point."

"Did you fight him?" Briggs asked.

"No, we just had a nice chat and I made it clear what would happen to him if he misbehaved. The demon understood perfectly."

Briggs stared at him. "Why would a demon listen to you?"

"Because I've killed plenty of them, many stronger than whatever this thing is and I'll happily add it to the list should it cause me problems. I'll get supper started."

"Sure, supper."

Danny left the still-gaping Briggs and went to do something really difficult: figure out how to turn on a magic stove.

◌

Briggs watched Ronin walk into the kitchen and gave a shake of his head. Who talked about killing demons as if it was no big deal? Not most humans and certainly not any beastfolk Briggs had ever met, yet Ronin said it like it was an ordinary thing. He looked down at the dagger in his hand. It had taken all Briggs had not to be swallowed up by Grimshadow.

He concentrated on the demon and a moment later found himself in the same dark space where they fought. The demon stared at him with its glowing red eyes but made no move to attack.

"What happened with you and Ronin?" Briggs asked.

"Is that the human's name? Such a terrifying being. Never in my eternal existence have I encountered such a person. Even my creator, a hellpriest of vast power, wouldn't hold a candle to this man. He could destroy me as easily as I might an imp. Please tell him I will obey his command and teach you the best ways to make use of my powers."

Briggs didn't know what to think. The savage, powerful creature he fought to barely a draw was nowhere to be found. This version of the demon was more like a well-trained hunting hound. While he certainly appreciated not having to worry about his body being taken over at any moment, he also felt a bit ambivalent about relying on someone else to help him secure the power he needed.

He pictured himself back in his body and he was. In the end, all that mattered was saving his pack. If Ronin's help made that easier, Briggs wasn't about to complain. His ego certainly wasn't so big that he'd refuse his new friend's help.

"Do you like carrots and parsnips?" Ronin asked from the kitchen.

"I've never eaten either, but I'm happy to try them." Briggs walked over and leaned in the kitchen doorway. Ronin had two big steaks sizzling in a pan and a bunch of sliced vegetables in another.

Briggs licked his lips. Those steaks looked even better than the sausages.

"I made you a small helping of vegetables," Ronin said.

"Thank you. Where did you have the steaks?"

"Are you familiar with a personal pocket dimension?"

Briggs shook his head. He'd never heard of such a thing. Magic wasn't something beastfolk had much use for.

"Basically it's a magic room where you can keep stuff and it won't spoil. Very handy for an adventurer." He flipped the steaks. "Will you start your training tomorrow?"

"Yes. I've never used a weapon like Grimshadow. It feels a bit awkward."

"Karambits can be tricky to use. The reach is awful but they're quick and maneuverable. Plus this one has a demon attached so I'm sure it'll give you some interesting abilities. Once you master the basics, I'd be happy to spar with you a bit."

"That would be helpful, thank you." Briggs hesitated then asked, "Why are you doing all this for me?"

Ronin cocked his head. "Why wouldn't I help you? I promised Val I'd do what I could to rescue the kidnapped beastfolk. You have the same goal. It's only natural that we work together. Besides, I can't read nonstop, my eyes would melt. Training with you will be a good break."

A white disk appeared in midair beside Ronin, who reached in and pulled out two wooden platters and two sets of utensils. He plated the steaks and vegetables then handed one to Briggs. The kitchen had a small table and they sat facing each other.

Briggs dug in and found the food delicious. Even the vegetables were crunchy and sweet. A few bites in Ronin snapped his fingers, reached into the disk and pulled out a flask and two cups.

"I'm afraid all I have to drink is water." He handed a full cup to Briggs.

"Water is all I've ever drank. Thank you."

Ronin nodded and got back to eating. They finished their meal in silence. When the last bite of steak was gone Briggs let out a long sigh. After all those weeks alone on the road, struggling to find enough food to survive, being able to eat his fill was like a dream.

"Finished?" Ronin asked.

"Yes, it was wonderful."

"Good." Ronin passed a hand over the platter, and some

magic left it completely clean. Once that was done, he put them back into his storage. "You can stay in the room next door. I don't know about you, but I could use some sleep."

Once Ronin said it, Briggs realized how tired he was. They left the kitchen and stepped out into the hall. Ronin showed him how to open and close the door of the room next to his and left him to his own devices. It didn't take long to find the bedroom and he lay down on the almost too soft bed. He stared up into the dark.

He didn't want to rely too much on Ronin. Rescuing his pack was Briggs's responsibility. He would find and kill all those responsible.

As the thought formed, he felt Grimshadow's eagerness. The demon's hunger for lives was even stronger than Briggs's appetite had been. Well, soon enough he would feed the demon all it could eat.

CHAPTER 7

The cold stone walls of the dimly lit basement chamber seemed to close in around Zane Latimer as he approached the black stone altar. His dark robe swished behind him as he walked, his mind cluttered with grim thoughts. His partner in Discourt had been slain and the project set back. An unfortunate turn of events to be sure.

He'd known, deep down, that relying on a nonbeliever to bring the plan to fruition was a mistake, but Avius had the technical expertise to alter the plague. Making the final tweak to increase its fatality rate had been a simple matter. But with Berend dead, he had no way of knowing what had happened in Discourt or the wider area.

People were still dying, which was good, though not nearly at the rate Zane would've liked. A disease was the perfect vector for Astaroth's curse since it required no agents to manage its spread. It was simply a matter of waiting then activating the ritual to raise the victims as an undead army.

Whines and whimpers mingled with the rattling of chains

brought him out of his musings. Thirty terrified slaves were chained to the walls on all sides of the black altar. Their wide, panicked eyes gleamed in the flickering torchlight. The air was thick with the stench of fear and despair. A lovely perfume.

Zane looked the wretched captives over. This should be enough to bring Berend back from Astaroth's hell. Zane had made arrangements for Berend's soul to receive a new host. The greater demon he'd bargained with was an especially evil specimen, but if he wanted to continue receiving his regular offerings of life force, he'd best live up to his end of the deal.

Well, time to get started.

Zane began his chant, ancient words of Infernal echoing off the stone as he moved with deliberate precision. The captives thrashed harder, struggling against the chains that held them tight. It was a pointless effort, but their desperation did strengthen the ambient corruption, so he appreciated it all the same.

He approached a sad-eyed woman of middle years first. She was nothing special, some farmer's wife the raiders had picked up. Maybe three small gold coins on the open market. No great loss to their finances.

Zane's dagger flashed, cutting her throat and sending blood gushing down the front of her torn smock. Her body slumped in its chains as her life force pooled above the altar.

One by one, he slaughtered them all, their life forces joining the pool. When the final slave was drained, he flicked the mingled blood across the altar and chanted the final line of the spell.

"Open the path to Astaroth's hell. Return, Berend, and serve once more."

A swirling vortex of black and crimson energy erupted from the altar top, the chill of its corruption a soothing caress to Zane's skin.

When the energy vanished, a single figure stood in its place. Berend was not the man he remembered. His time in Astaroth's hell had left him changed. Hints of who he'd been remained. The bald head, thin features, and sharp gaze were still there. Only now two short, jutting horns poked out of Berend's forehead. Instead of merely being thin, he was gaunt to the point of skeletal. And the sharp gaze came from glowing red eyes.

Zane would never criticize his master's aesthetic, but it would be difficult for Berend to blend in looking like this. But that's what magic was for.

"Berend," Zane said. "How did you enjoy your time in the master's hell?"

"It left something to be desired, especially that pig of a demon you left my soul with. I'd expected better treatment given my years of service."

"You would've gotten it under different circumstances. I needed the demon to keep your soul contained so you wouldn't merge with the essence of Hell. Had that happened, much of your personality and memories would've been lost, which would've defeated the purpose of calling you back."

"Well, I am back, so I suppose I can't complain too loudly. How long have I been dead?"

"A month or so. Let's go upstairs. The others are waiting to hear how the finest swordsman any of us have ever seen ended up the first of the group slain."

Zane led the way out of the altar chamber. He had no fear of leaving Berend at his back. The newly born demon was incapable of betraying his summoner. He'd woven that restriction into the spell. Along with several other precautions should his ally decide to rebel.

At the top of a rough set of stone stairs they entered the fortress proper. There were no living servants to be found, only minor demonic spirits and undead. Normal humans not affiliated with Astaroth wouldn't do well at their fortress. The corruption would, at a minimum, leave them weak and shaken.

They turned down a shadowy passage which led to the fortress's great hall. The two remaining members of the group, Nash Veil, the blind swordsman, and Voss White, necromancer and all around lunatic, sat at a long black table engraved with Astaroth's skull.

Nash wore black leather armor and kept a slim, curved sword at his side. His expression was impassive, but it was a rare person that could meet the gaze of his empty eye sockets.

Voss, on the other hand, wore pure-white robes nearly as pale as his skin. A staff of bleached bone rested on the table beside him.

Voss held out a hand to Nash. "Told you it would work."

Despite his lack of eyes, Nash dropped a jingling pouch into Voss's hand.

"You had doubts, Nash?" Zane asked, his tone sharp.

"Only about the size of your sacrifice." Nash's voice was completely calm. "I thought you'd need more. Welcome back, Berend."

"Nash, Voss, been a while since we all met face to face," Berend said.

"And what a face." Voss chuckled. "Did the master's hell disagree with you?"

"Shut up, Voss. No one thinks your foolishness is amusing." Zane sat at the head of the table while Berend took the spot to his right, beside Nash. "Now, why don't you tell us how you ended up in your current state."

"That's easy enough," Berend said. "I fought an adventurer named Ronin. Just a kid, barely made elite a few months ago. Should've been an easy kill."

When Berend trailed off Zane said, "But?"

"But it wasn't. He was strong and fast. I couldn't touch him. It was over in moments. He took me out along with six top mercenaries like we were goblins armed with clubs. The whole fight lasted less than a minute. Next thing I know I'm in the master's hell with that demon picking at my soul like it was a scab."

"He did provide you with a proper new body," Zane said.

"Eventually."

"Is it strong enough to kill this adventurer?" Zane asked.

"I don't know," Berend said with obvious reluctance. "Based on our first fight, I'm not optimistic."

"You're a demon for hell's sake," Voss said. "Surely no adventurer is strong enough to fight someone with your skill in an immortal body."

"You might be right," Berend said. "But I'm not sure and that worries me."

Zane waved a hand. "The adventurer isn't a priority. However strong he is or isn't, I'm certain he's far from here. Of more immediate concern is the plague's spread. It's slowed to almost nothing. Berend's last report regarding Avius's search for a way to undo the alteration I made is troubling. If he succeeds, we won't have enough raw material for a proper army."

"He won't," Berend said. "The fool has been working nonstop and made no noticeable progress. The towns have learned to keep strangers out until the priests can confirm they're healthy, that's what's holding the spread down. Once trading season picks up, so should the spread."

"I hope you're right," Zane said. "Now that we've lost our eyes in Discourt, I have no idea what's going on with the temples. The archangels' servants have proven far too adept at undoing the master's plans. We need information."

"Send one of the cure merchants." Nash had been so quiet Zane almost forgot he was present. "No one would give them a second glance."

"Not a bad idea," Zane said. "But they don't know us. Berend is the only one they're likely to listen to willingly and he doesn't exactly look like he used to."

Voss snorted. "A glamour spell will fix that. If you find the merchants, I'll have Berend back to his ugly old self in no time."

Zane nodded. "Agreed."

"There's one problem," Voss said.

Zane bit back a scathing reply. "Go on."

"I'm out of ether crystals. If you want the magic to last longer than a few hours, I'll need one to power a spell generator."

"Nash can get it for you," Zane said.

"Can't you send Berend?" Nash asked. "I hate Vulmar and his thugs. It's a struggle not to kill them all every time I visit the miserable hole."

"Berend would draw too much attention as he is now. You're our best option, so spare me your complaints." Zane looked around the table, his gaze resting on each of them for a moment before moving on. "Let's get to work. For Astaroth's glory."

"For Astaroth's glory," they echoed.

CHAPTER 8

Danny had been reading for eight hours a day the last three days and his eyes were bitter about being so overworked. They itched, stung, and watered depending on their mood. On the plus side, Danny had worked his way through four dry, tedious technical manuals written by different elf-blood wizards. The books must've been intended for fellow wizards since few explanations for the esoteric terms were provided.

But at last his patience had paid off. At the back of his current book was a map showing locations of all the ether pools and the ethereal lines connecting them to Elfhome. It was quite detailed given its size. Copying it wouldn't be a speedy task. And, while he doubted anyone would care if he just took the original, he preferred to leave it behind as a precaution. If the worst happened and the copy ended up destroyed, he could return and make another.

How he was going to deal with something so huge was another matter altogether. Knowing where the ether pools were did him no good if he couldn't find a way to disrupt them.

"Right, one thing at a time." It was still winter after all. No sense rushing out to freeze on the road. Best to find all the information he could before he left. The last thing Danny wanted to do was backtrack ten thousand miles because he missed some vital detail.

With the tip of his finger he traced the lines from each ether pool. They all ran straight to Elfhome. That being the case, how the hell did the cathedral end up as the spell's focus? Adonael created the cathedral, maybe the archangel extended the line as well.

He couldn't decide if it mattered and his indecision annoyed him.

Time for a break. The tightness in his back made it clear he'd been sitting in his chair for too long.

Danny grinned as he stood and stretched. "Librarian."

The ghostly, hooded figure came gliding out from the stacks. Danny had no way of telling what the faceless demon was thinking, but he liked to imagine the interruption annoyed it. He couldn't say why, but the idea amused him.

When the librarian stopped a few feet away Danny asked, "Can you make me a copy of this map?"

The cowled head shifted from Danny to the map and back. "I'm a librarian, not your personal secretary."

"I thought you were supposed to help me in whatever way I needed. I'm not the best artist in the world and I thought you could do a better job copying this than I'd ever manage. Was I mistaken? Perhaps we could ask the Reaper to decide."

Danny felt a little bad. He was basically threatening to

complain to the manager. It wasn't a very nice thing to do, but he was bored and needed some entertainment.

"Fine, but so you know, this is why demons hate humans."

"Really? Do many humans ask you to copy maps from ancient elvish books of magic? That's a very specific thing to hate humans for."

"I hate humans for reasons both general and specific," the librarian said. "Give me the book and a few hours. I'll have your copy ready. Now that you have a map, I assume you'll be leaving soon."

"Not terribly soon. I have a lot more research to do. I'll be counting on you."

The demon grumbled something no doubt unkind, collected the book, and glided off. Danny didn't know what you tipped a demon, but he felt like he should give the librarian something for the laugh.

Maybe Riko would know more about how the summoning spell's focus was shifted. At a minimum, looking for her would get him out of the library for a while. Danny found the prospect very appealing.

He descended to the first floor and stepped outside into the fresh air. It was a beautiful winter day. The sky was bright blue, with hardly a cloud to be seen. It didn't feel quite as cold as it had been lately either. Perhaps the worst of it had gone by.

"Riko!" he said, his voice seeming far too loud in the silent city. "I need to talk to you!"

Moments later, a dark shape came soaring down. Riko landed beside him, her red eyes gleaming in the fading light, and folded her wings behind her.

"Is all well, Ronin?" she asked.

"As well as it can be. I had a question. I know Adonael

created the Crystal Cathedral so I assume she also moved the ethereal line. Is that right?"

"She used her power of creation to extend the ethereal line rather than move it, but you're basically correct. That's why the summoning ritual is so much weaker now."

Danny frowned. Dragging someone's soul out of their body and pulling it heaven knew how far across reality seemed pretty strong to him.

"Would you like to see it?" she asked.

"The line? I thought it was underground, like some kind of magic power cable."

"It is, but we can still go take a look. The tunnel has plenty of extra space."

Curiosity got the better of Danny and he said, "Sure, lead the way."

Riko led Danny back inside the central tower. Off to one side, in a shadowy alcove, she pressed her palm against the smooth metal wall. A hidden rune appeared, flashed once, and a door dropped into the floor. Behind it, a dark staircase spiraled down into the earth.

A glowing red light appeared above Riko's head and she started down. He followed her into the depths. Minutes dragged by and Danny was starting to wonder how deep they were going.

The thought had barely formed when the staircase ended at what looked like a cave entrance. From within, a golden glow emerged.

A single stride carried him into the cave, which turned out to be a tunnel. The ethereal line stretched as far as he could see in either direction. Nearly as big around as Danny was tall, it would've worked fine as a sewer pipe. Only the golden lightning streaking down it nonstop ruined the image.

"Impressive, isn't it?" she asked.

"Yeah. Can it be severed?"

"With magic all things are possible. The master could do it with a thought. We, on the other hand, are far more limited beings."

Great, he just needed the power of a demon lord. Shouldn't be a problem.

"Step back. It probably won't do any good, but I'll kick myself if I don't at least try." Danny reached into storage and pulled out the ethersword.

He lit it as Riko moved to the bottom step. Channeling all the power he could muster, Danny swung.

The glowing white blade crashed into the line and bounced off without so much as denting it. There was no backlash or discomfort and the sword appeared unaffected by the blow.

The ethereal line went right on doing what it did, seemingly unaware of his presence. If it had been a living thing he would've been offended at being ignored. As it was Danny just felt depressed. This was going to be so much harder than he first thought.

"Don't despair," Riko said. "This is the largest line. It carries the converged energy of all the ether pools to the cathedral. The others will only be five percent as large."

Danny took some comfort in that. Not a lot, but it was better than nothing. "Let's go back. I have more reading to do."

Hopefully he could find a better plan than trying to cut it with a magic sword.

CHAPTER 9

Danny clonked his way up the stairs. He still couldn't believe the ethereal line didn't so much as flex when he hit it. A blow like the one he struck would cut most demons in half. He swallowed a sigh. Plenty of people had warned him he had no chance of destroying the summoning spell, but this was the first time he thought they might be right.

Not that he was going to give up on his mission. Anything that could be made could be destroyed. He'd find a way. There were plenty of books on the subject he hadn't even glanced at waiting in the library. One of them would tell him what he needed to know.

Hopefully.

Ahead of him, Riko flew silently along. She didn't beat her wings, which confirmed her flying ability was magical. He'd figured it was. The anatomy was all wrong for her to fly without magic.

He shook his head at the stupid distraction. Danny didn't want to think about his failure and there was nothing else to it. But he needed to think about it. Things had been going his way for a while now. He couldn't let this setback shake his determination.

At last they emerged into the tower's entry hall. Briggs was pacing not far from the door, his new dagger clutched in his hand. Danny hadn't seen the kid except for mealtimes, so finding him waiting was a surprise.

"Ronin!" Briggs hurried over. "Toad said you were here. I've been practicing. Do you think we could spar a little?"

"Sure. I've been sitting on my ass nonstop the last three days. A little exercise sounds like just the thing. Let's step outside."

"Who's Toad?" Riko asked.

Briggs turned so he was running backwards. "It's the name I gave the demon you assigned as my guide. It looks like a toad, so I figured that's what I'd call it."

Briggs grinned, turned back, and kept running toward the door. So much youthful energy. Who was Danny kidding? His host body wasn't much older than Briggs. His lack of energy was mental, not physical.

"He's doing much better with Grimshadow than I expected," Riko said.

"Yeah, I had a chat with the demon and explained what would happen if he was less than helpful with Briggs's training. I'm glad he got the message."

"You spoke to Grimshadow?" Riko sounded surprised.

"Yup. He made some typical demon threats, no offense, and I responded by telling him I'd shred his essence to nothing if he made my life difficult. Seems he believed me. Which is good, since I meant every word. Why were you surprised?"

"Grimshadow is one of the stronger demonic spirits

serving the master on this world. I doubted he would be intimidated by anyone. Apparently I overestimated him."

"What did the Reaper tell you about me?" Danny asked.

"Not a lot beyond the fact that you were summoned from the same Earth where I lived and that I was to help you in any way you required."

"Do you know about the demon king?" Danny asked.

"Of course. The master's will fight in the final round of the game. Why?"

"I beat Ardent Lilly's demon king in this round. Though she managed to resurrect herself somewhere so maybe it doesn't count as a complete win. Anyway, I did defeat her in battle if that gives you some idea of how I stack up."

Riko's jaw dropped. "You beat a demon king?"

Danny nodded. "She was tough and it was a near thing, but yes, I did."

Briggs had gotten well ahead of him so Danny picked up the pace a bit, leaving the still-stunned Riko to bring up the rear.

The kid had his dagger in a reverse grip, his index finger through the opening at the end of the karambit's hilt. His stance was low and balanced as he bounced on the balls of his feet. Looked like he'd figured out how to hold it properly anyway.

Danny drew his sword and wrapped it in an ethereal sheath to make sure he didn't accidentally hurt Briggs. Next he added speed and strength enhancements along with a barrier just in case.

"Ready?" Danny asked.

"Whenever you are," Briggs said.

"Riko, would you give us a countdown please?" Danny asked.

The demon moved off to one side and raised her hand. "Three, two, one!"

Briggs lunged, far faster than any normal person.

Of course there was fast and then there was Danny. He dodged easily and slapped Briggs on the back with the flat of his sword as he passed.

Briggs skidded to a stop and spun to face Danny, his mouth hanging open. "How…?"

"You're pretty quick," Danny said. "I doubt many people could keep up with you now. I just happen to be one of them. Want to try your defense?"

"What—" Briggs barely got the word out before Danny exploded into motion.

He darted past Briggs, poked the kid in the ribs, spun, darted behind him as he turned, and poked him on the other side before leaping back and stopping.

Briggs rubbed his sides. "I couldn't even see you move. How fast were you going?"

"About half my maximum. I can hold back more if you want to go again. I wasn't sure how much you could handle and I wanted to be sure to give you a challenge."

"I definitely feel challenged." He blew out a sigh. "I thought I'd be able to keep up with you for sure. So much for that idea."

"It's only been a few days," Danny said. "Be patient and keep at it. Also, and I don't mean this in an arrogant way, but I'm stronger than pretty much anyone you're likely to meet. I might not be the best person to compare yourself to."

"Ronin has a point," Riko said. "You should try going into the forest and hunting some of the demonic beasts. They would make a much more realistic challenge for you. Sparring with someone isn't the same as trying to kill them. You can't really give it your all."

Danny glanced at the demon, surprised by her thoughtful reply. "She's right. Plus, if you bring back some hide, we could finally make you a sheath."

"But no meat," Riko said. "Corrupted beasts are inedible."

Briggs perked up. "I've never hunted in a forest. It should be fun. Thanks for the lesson."

"Will you be back for supper?" Danny asked.

"I'll try to be," Briggs said. "But if I'm late, I can eat whatever you fix cold. See you."

Briggs trotted off toward the forest.

Danny turned to Riko. "That was good advice. I never thought about sparring in exactly those terms."

"I can't claim the advice as my own. When I was a living woman, my sisters and I trained all the time, but our grand-master always cautioned us it was different when your life was on the line. I just paraphrased what she told us over and over."

"Well, wherever it came from, I'm glad you decided to share. I've got more reading to do. Good afternoon." Danny headed back to the central tower. It was time to stick his nose back in a book.

Briggs walked down the dirt street, head hanging. He'd been so sure he could beat Ronin or at least keep up with him. Briggs had never felt anything like the magic his new dagger possessed. It made him feel invincible.

A little frown creased his face. Invincible? What a joke.

And maybe it was just as well to find out in a fight with his friend rather than an enemy. He sighed and looked up into the clear blue sky.

Could he save his pack if this was all he could manage against Ronin?

Comparing yourself to that terrifying human is a fool's errand. I warned you about that before you approached him, but you ignored me.

Briggs still wasn't used to hearing that cold voice in his mind. "I had to know, to see where I stood. My distaste for the answer doesn't mean anything."

I still have a few tricks to teach you, but even when you master everything I can do, you'll still have no chance of beating him. Best if you accept that now.

"I know, I know. Believe me, I do. I suppose it's lucky I don't have to fight Ronin to rescue my pack."

It's a good thing you don't have to fight him for any reason. I have no desire to spend centuries waiting for another bearer.

Briggs swallowed a humorless laugh. Grimshadow didn't pull his punches.

When he reached the edge of the forest, Briggs took a deep breath and banished thoughts of his loss. A hunter had to focus fully on his prey if he was to succeed. Or so the pack's hunt master used to say.

As soon as Briggs strode into the forest, the air grew thick and still. A different sort of chill made his hackles rise.

Demonic corruption. Without the human's magic protecting you, you're forced to endure the full effect.

The good news never stopped. "Then we'd best finish this hunt as quickly as possible. Can you guide me to a boar? My usual means of hunting are useless with all these trees blocking my view."

Grimshadow's cold presence slid into Briggs's consciousness and he immediately sensed all the life around him. It all felt wrong.

No normal animal would ever come this close to the master's temple. You will find nothing within several miles save demonic and corrupt beasts as well as our guardian demons. The latter won't trouble you since you're a guest of the master.

"What's the difference between a corrupted beast and a demonic one?" Briggs asked.

A demonic beast is one that houses a demon spirit. A corrupt beast is a normal beast that has been transformed by the ambient corruption. The second is weaker than the first.

All this demon business was giving Briggs a headache. "Just find me the right prey to hunt."

One of the presences he sensed grew stronger and Briggs understood that was the one he wanted. Grimshadow guided Briggs deeper into the corrupted forest. The unnatural stillness pressed in on him from all sides. Only the faintest breeze rustling the leaves broke the silence.

As his prey got closer, Briggs dropped into a crouch. He moved downwind of his quarry, careful not to make a sound. When he sensed the target only yards away he dropped to his stomach and crawled the final few feet.

He peeked around a tree and spotted a huge boar. Its eyes glowed with an eerie red light, duller than Riko's but no less unsettling. Black ichor oozed from cracks in its leathery hide and the stench of rot filled the air around it.

A demonic boar. Be cautious. Its hide will be tougher than an ordinary boar and its tusks are poisonous.

Briggs had never hunted a boar of any sort and had no idea how tough they might be. But tough or not, he was determined to defeat it.

He crept closer, every sense alert.

Fifteen yards away, the boar snorted and spun, staring right at him.

It sensed your life force.

Briggs leapt to his feet. "You didn't say it could do that."

Not all of them can. Get ready.

He shifted Grimshadow to guard position and watched the boar. He didn't have long to wait.

The boar charged, its hooves churning the forest floor and sending clods of dirt flying.

Briggs leapt to the side at the last second, slashing with Grimshadow as the boar passed. The blade cut a shallow gash in the beast's flank. Black ichor spurted out, sizzling where it struck the ground.

The boar skidded to a halt and spun around, red eyes blazing. It lowered its head, pawed the ground, and charged again.

Briggs stood his ground until the last possible heartbeat.

Time slowed.

He vaulted over the boar's back, twisting in midair to land on its neck, and plunged Grimshadow deep into the beast's skull.

The blade sank in to the hilt.

The boar screamed, an earsplitting shriek that hurt Briggs's ears. He twisted the blade from side to side, cutting the wound wider.

A shudder ran through its body and the boar collapsed. Through his connection to Grimshadow, Briggs knew it was dead.

He blew out a breath and wiped the sweat from his brow.

Well done. I thought it might give you more trouble. Its corrupt life force wasn't the finest meal, but given how long it's been, I won't complain.

Briggs's grin turned to a grimace as he watched the black ooze leaking out of the boar. He wasn't sure he wanted to use its hide for a sheath.

We'll hunt something more suitable next time. Best return to the city. The really strong things come out at night.

It seemed wrong to abandon his kill, but there was nothing he could make use of. And Briggs wasn't eager to find out what Grimshadow considered really strong.

Not tonight at least. But eventually he'd have to face the worst this forest had to offer. It would be his rite of passage. Then he'd know it was time to hunt the slavers who took his pack.

CHAPTER 10

Nash Veil strode down the rough dirt street running through the center of a mining camp built at the base of the Crystal Mist Mountains. His boots crunched in the gravel and mud. A recent snowstorm had left the town's lone street a sodden mess. He hated it here, but there was nowhere else to get the ether crystals Voss needed to power his magic.

And Nash, as the most normal looking of the group now that Berend had been transformed into a demon, was stuck with the job. Best to complete his task as quickly as possible and return to the fortress.

His empty eye sockets scanned the first of two makeshift bunkhouses built from scavenged boards and piled-up mine tailings that sat on the side of the road. Magic allowed Nash to see more clearly than most people with eyes and what he saw didn't impress him. There were only three nice buildings in the village: the crystal refinery, Boss Vulmar's house, and the camp's tavern which served to separate the slave-keepers from their wages. The keepers lived in a slightly better bunkhouse that a generous man might call an oversized shack.

Today, Nash's destination was Vulmar's house. The obese half-ogre ran everything in the town with surprising skill and unsurprising brutality. Some would no doubt find Nash's distaste amusing given his worship of the Lord of the Undead, but Nash had his reasons for joining forces with Zane and he cared not in the least what anyone thought about his choices.

The house itself was two stories of stonework with glass windows and a tile roof. Two armed guards, both half-ogres —all Vulmar's men were of the same lineage—stood on either side of the path leading to the front door. They wore leather vests and trousers and seemed wholly untroubled by the cold. Each guard held a double-bitted ax that a human would've struggled to lift.

They eyed Nash as he approached, their grips tightening on their axes. When it was clear Nash wasn't turning off, the one on the right held up a hand. "The boss isn't seeing no one today. Come back tomorrow."

Nash had no intention of spending a moment longer in this backwater dump than absolutely necessary. "He'll see me. Go tell Vulmar that Nash Veil wishes to speak with him."

The left-hand guard snorted. "Don't matter who you are. If we bother the boss, he'll kill us."

Nash brushed his cloak aside to make drawing his sword easier. "What makes you think I won't?"

The guards looked at each other, brows furrowed. Perhaps the question was too difficult for them.

The left-hand guard swung back and raised his ax.

In a single fluid motion Nash drew his sword and sliced

through both of the guard's wrists, sending his ax, hands and all, crashing to the ground.

He had his blade at the second guard's throat an instant later. "Go tell Vulmar that Nash Veil wishes to speak with him. I won't ask again."

The guard tossed his ax aside and ran for the house. Nash stepped over the pool of blood soaking the dirt and followed along behind, returning his sword to its sheath as he did.

He despised dealing with thugs and fools. Pity the world was overpopulated with them. Hopefully Zane's undead army would be more reasonable once they rose.

The guard scrambled through the door and into the house. Nash waited for him on the porch that wrapped all the way around the building, his ethereal eyes allowing him to survey all of Vulmar's gloomy domain. Why anyone would want to live here was beyond him. The only possibility that made sense was the village's superiority to wherever Vulmar and his thugs came from.

The fact that such a place might exist depressed Nash to no end. His sense of beauty nearly demanded that he find the place and wipe it off the face of the world. Pity he didn't have the time at the moment.

A shout and roar from inside confirmed the guard had located his employer.

Half a minute later Vulmar himself came stomping out the door. He had nothing save a loincloth covering him. His pebbly green skin strained to contain his massive gut. Four distinct chins hid his thick neck.

Nash nearly killed him for the crime of being so ugly.

"You have horrible timing," Vulmar said. "This is my day off."

"Calling it your day off implies you have days where you work. I've yet to see any evidence to support such a claim."

Vulmar grimaced, his body tensing.

"Don't make me kill you," Nash said, his voice impassive. "I have no idea who your second-in-command is and I have equally little interest in looking for him."

Vulmar relaxed a fraction. "What do you want? As if I don't know."

"I need five crystals, at least one inch across and ninety percent clarity."

"Five hundred, each."

Nash said nothing.

The silence stretched to the breaking point. Nash kept his empty eye sockets focused on Vulmar until the latter looked away.

"You're costing me a fortune here," Vulmar said.

Nash shook his head. "You're mistaken. We're allowing you to make a fortune. It's more convenient for us to let you handle the mine. We could have Zane's undead dig out the crystals and process them ourselves, but it takes time better spent on other things. You get to sell the crystals we don't need. How is it you don't understand your place in this arrangement?"

Vulmar ground his teeth hard enough for Nash's sensitive hearing to pick it up. "You need me."

Nash shook his head again. "Would you like me to show you just how little we need you or do you want to get me the crystals I came for so I can leave this cesspool you call a camp? Decide quickly. It's too cold to stand around glaring at each other."

Vulmar barked a laugh. "You can't glare without eyes. Come on, they're in the processing center."

The half-ogre stomped, barefoot, through the nearly frozen mud. Nash followed, careful to keep enough distance between them to avoid getting splashed.

"Would it kill you to wear a blindfold or something?" Vulmar asked. "Those empty eye sockets of yours give me the creeps."

"I couldn't possible care less what you think about my lack of eyes. If they trouble you, it's your problem, not mine."

"I hate you, have I told you that before?"

"You might have. I can say with complete honesty that I've forgotten every word you've spoken to me before this visit, and I'll happily forget everything you say to me today as quickly as possible after I leave."

Vulmar let out a little growl and picked up his pace.

The processing center was a squat stone building, its chimney belching smoke into the cold mountain air. Vulmar shoved open the heavy wooden door and marched inside, leaving muddy footprints on the floor. The workers, a mixture of beastfolk and human slaves, toiled to extract the ether crystals from the raw ore mined deep beneath the mountains.

Nash followed silently behind. The warmth was almost shocking after the cold outside. He was surprised Vulmar allowed the slaves this much comfort.

The slaves didn't even look up as they passed. Their total concentration was on carefully chiseling away rock to free the glowing ether crystals. Four half-ogre slavedrivers watched over them, whips coiled at their belts in silent threat.

Vulmar led Nash to a room at the back. With a grunt, he opened the iron-banded door and went inside.

The room wasn't huge, little more than a large closet

really, with shelves lining the walls. A dozen leather pouches sat on the shelves. In the center, a large wooden table took up the bulk of the space, its surface scarred from years of sorting and grading the precious gemstones.

Vulmar lumbered over to one of the shelves and grabbed a pouch. His thick fingers were surprisingly nimble as he fished out five crystals.

"Five of the best we have in stock."

Nash took one and let the ether flow through it and back to him. The quality was acceptable.

"These will do. I'll be on my way so you can resume enjoying your day off."

Vulmar grunted and led him back into the street. They parted ways without further conversation. Nash would travel through the night. Darkness was no obstacle for a blind man after all.

Once Berend had his disguise, he could come collect whatever crystals they needed. If Nash never had to visit this place again it would suit him very well.

CHAPTER 11

D anny squinted at the faded pages, the musty smell of ancient parchment filling his nose. His head throbbed and his vision blurred, but he refused to stop. He was almost finished with his current book and he wanted to get through it before heading upstairs to start supper.

He swallowed a sigh. How long had he been reading? Inside the windowless library time meant nothing. The light never changed and neither did the temperature. He might've been in another dimension. Only his occasionally grumbling stomach reminding him when it was time for the next meal gave him a sense of how long he'd been at it.

That and the burning in his eyes. The many days of practice had him able to maintain the translation spell for ten hours if he really pushed himself. It would also leave him nearly blind for an hour, so he didn't do that anymore.

He flipped to the next page and found a detailed illustration of an ether pool. In the center of a circle it simply read

Concentrated Ether. All around the circle were intricate symbols and runes.

Danny hurried down to the dense blocks of script below the image. He recognized the writing, having seen it here and there in several other books. It was from the head wizard on the project, a half-elf of the high council.

Danny's pulse quickened as he read.

The precision of the runes is paramount. Even the slightest disruption will drain the ether pool entirely. Even worse, the pool will be unable to refill until the runes are repaired. Despite all my efforts to make the spell more robust, there is no way around this. Utmost care must be taken to ensure the circle's protection.

Danny sat back and ran a hand through his hair. If he could damage the rune circle and drain the ether pool, it was unlikely anyone living had the knowledge and skill to fix them. The protections, on the other hand, might be a problem.

Who was he kidding? Wards and guardians created by the elf-bloods would absolutely be a problem, but if he could make it past them, he had hope for success. After his failure with the ethereal line, he'd been less than optimistic for a while. Not that Danny was the sort to linger on negative emotions.

He rubbed his eyes, renewed his spell, and got back to it.

Given the weakness of the rune circle, redundancies will be necessary. My recommendation to the council was to double the number of ether pools. That will double the amount of time needed to finish the project, but it will also ensure that, even if half of them are damaged, our forces will have a way to come and go from the new world. Hopefully the rest of the council will agree to my proposal.

Having seen the map of the complete ritual, Danny knew

the council had agreed. There were twenty ether pools marked on the map, which meant he needed to damage eleven of them at minimum to ensure Earth's safety.

Heaven's mercy, that was a lot. And in the end, he didn't know for sure that Adonael wouldn't be able to instruct her servants on how to fix them. The archangels didn't usually interfere directly, but sharing information was kind of a gray area. There didn't seem to be a rule, they just did whatever they thought best in the moment.

Danny sighed and closed the book. There was no sense worrying about it. He'd done about all he could with research. It was time to find the nearest ether pool and take a look at it.

Once he had firsthand knowledge of them, he could return and do more research should it be necessary. At least he assumed he could. Before he left, he'd have to talk to Riko and make sure he'd be welcome to return.

But that would keep until later. For today, it was time for supper and then a good night's sleep. Tomorrow he'd talk to his hostess and, assuming he got good news, he'd set out for the nearest ether pool.

Danny snapped his fingers. He also needed to talk to Briggs about his plans. The kid had been training nonstop since their sparring match the other day. Danny wasn't sure if he'd be welcome here on his own.

He fought a yawn and lost. Right, tomorrow. All of that would keep until tomorrow.

Briggs's feet felt like they weighed about ten pounds each as he climbed the final steps up to the third floor of the central tower. He'd done little beyond train for the last couple days and had at last mastered Grimshadow's final ability, a short-range teleportation spell. It was a useful ability but limited. Briggs could only use it twice every hour.

Still, using it—along with invisibility and an obscuring mist—had allowed him to take down a pair of demonic ogres all by himself. A little more practice and he felt confident he'd be ready to resume the search for his pack.

Best give yourself at least another week. Learning to use my abilities isn't something to be done halfheartedly.

He nodded but was too tired to argue.

On the third-floor landing he caught the scent of roasting meat and spices from Ronin's room. His mouth watered. Everything the human cooked was delicious and Briggs was starving.

He knocked then pressed the rune that made the door slide into the floor. "Ronin?"

From the kitchen Ronin said, "Come in and sit down. I'm almost done."

Briggs crossed the entry area and joined his friend in the kitchen. He glanced into the frying pan Ronin was stirring. It looked like two different sorts of meat mixed together.

"What's that?"

"A special treat, sausage and hamburger mixed together. I think you'll enjoy it."

Briggs sat at the little table in the kitchen and picked up his fork.

Ronin made two plates and poured two cups of water for

them before joining him at the table. He set the plate in front of Briggs who immediately started eating.

Halfway through the meal Ronin said, "I've found the information I needed in the library. Tomorrow morning I'm leaving Elfhome for the nearest ether pool. I'll talk to Riko about letting you stay and continue training. You'll have to do your own cooking from now on."

Briggs didn't register much after Ronin said he was leaving. His fork froze halfway to his mouth as he tried to make sense of what he just heard.

At last he said, "Where are you going?"

"Northeast, the target was built under some mountains. The Crystal Mists, I believe, is the name of the range. It's a few hundred miles from here."

"Northeast is the direction the slavers were taking my pack. Are the mountains near the slaver villages?"

"I'm not sure. The map doesn't have much detail on local settlements. Not to mention it's over fifteen hundred years old. Heaven knows how accurate it is now."

"I'll come with you," Briggs said. "If your path brings you close to the villages, we can, how did you put it, kill two birds with one stone."

Ronin grinned. "It's your call. If you want to come with me, you're welcome. I'm not in such a big rush that I won't take the time to keep my promise to Val."

Briggs stared at his plate. "I thought you might argue."

"Why?"

"I did so poorly in our sparring match…"

"Look, I think I've been clear about where I stand. You have to make your own decisions. As your friend, my job is to support you, not argue with you. If you're ready to try and find your pack, I'll do what I can to help."

"Thanks, Ronin, that means a lot."

"Sure. Now finish your supper and get some sleep. We've got a busy day tomorrow."

Briggs wouldn't let a scrap of meat go to waste, but he wouldn't be going to bed. If he was going to begin his quest for revenge in earnest, he needed to make sure he could do it.

Tonight he would hunt the most powerful demonic beast in the forest and either it would die, or he would.

CHAPTER 12

Briggs left Ronin's room and blew out a sigh as he turned toward the steps rather than his own cozy bed. Tired as he was, he couldn't rest now. He'd learned to use all of Grimshadow's abilities, but he wasn't sure he'd truly mastered them.

This would be the final test before he resumed his search.

This is a bad idea. You're still exhausted from the day's training.

"I'm surprised you care."

I don't especially care about you, but I have no wish to end up in that empty room for centuries waiting for someone else to show up. You're far from an ideal bearer, but you are better than nothing.

"Thanks."

He reached the ground floor and stepped out into the chilly night air. The worst of the cold seemed to be behind them now and soon the ground would soften and mud season would begin. It seldom bothered the pack when they were on the plains, but in human lands he was less confident about what effect it might have.

But mud was the least of Briggs's worries tonight.

He set out for the forest's edge. There was one section he'd been avoiding during his previous hunts. There was a powerful, corrupt presence there, but it never seemed active during the day. Briggs felt certain it had to be the strongest demonic beast in the forest.

It is. If you're determined to do this at least do it smart. Collapse your presence like I taught you so the beast doesn't sense our approach.

"Invisibility as well?" Briggs asked.

No need for that. It'll smell or sense you before it sees you. Best to save your strength for the fight.

Briggs focused inward, imagining himself shrinking into a tiny speck, imperceptible to the world around him. Despite doing exactly what Grimshadow told him, there was no way to know if it had worked until he was within range of the demon beast. And by then it would be too late to try again.

Well, a hunter couldn't succeed without courage. Briggs set out through the shadowed trees, and only the faint crunch of his boots on the half-frozen ground marked his passage.

The corrupt presence grew gradually stronger. The foul energy made his nose wrinkle and the hair on his arms stand up. He slowed his pace, each step deliberate and silent as he scanned the darkness. Moonlight filtered down through the barren branches, deepening the shadows.

A shape detached from the gloom. It had to be at least fifteen feet tall. Once-brown hair fell out in clumps and malevolent red eyes gleamed as the demonic beast prowled into a shaft of pale light.

Briggs had seen a bear once. The huge beast had run down an antelope and killed it with a single blow of its three-inch claws. This thing was twice as big as that bear. Serrated fangs jutted from its jaws and spines bristled along its back.

It hasn't sensed your presence yet. You can still retreat.

Maybe he could've, but Briggs had no intention of backing down. He couldn't. He needed to do this to prove to himself he was ready to take the next step.

Briggs drew in a slow breath, letting it out without a sound. He flexed his fingers before easing Grimshadow out of the crude sheath he and Ronin had made.

No sign that the demon bear had noticed him.

Good.

He crept closer, each step measured, making no sound. Just a little further and he'd have the perfect angle to strike. He had to go for its head. No shallow slash would stop this monster.

His muscles coiled, ready to spring.

The bear's head swung toward him. Crimson eyes locked on his own.

It roared and reared up on its back legs. Briggs's target was now way beyond his reach. Looked like he was going to have to do this the hard way.

Briggs lunged, Grimshadow leading.

He rolled under the bear's first swipe and slashed it across the belly before darting back out of range.

His horror grew as the deep slash healed in moments. As he feared, only an instantly fatal blow would do the job. The trick was going to be getting it.

The demon bear roared, its fury shaking the trees and making Briggs's knees wobble.

That's a magical effect. It's trying to root you in place. I negated the worst of it. Watch out!

The beast lunged at Briggs with terrifying speed.

Briggs dodged by the narrowest of margins.

The bear didn't let up. It spun, claws rushing through the air, seeking to rend him limb from limb.

Briggs danced back, slashing again and again, opening gashes that healed almost as quickly as he made them. Black blood matted the bear's fur, but it showed no sign of pain or slowing.

Briggs panted, his muscles burning as he evaded another brutal swipe. The demon bear was relentless, giving him no opening to launch a counterattack. He needed to change tactics or this fight would be over before it truly began.

He feinted left, then dove right as the bear lunged. Tucking into a roll, he felt the whoosh of displaced air as the massive paw passed inches from his head.

Briggs sprang to his feet behind the beast and activated Grimshadow's teleportation ability.

An instant later he appeared on the bear's back right behind its head.

The bear roared, bucking and twisting, trying to throw him off. Briggs hung on with one hand and hammered Grimshadow into its neck and skull. Even the demonic blade skipped off the bear's massive skull.

The beast thrashed, nearly throwing him off. Briggs dug his knees into its matted fur, barely keeping his seat. He couldn't keep this up much longer.

Briggs steadied himself as the bear bucked again. It paused for a second and he struck with all his might.

Grimshadow sank deep into the bear's skull.

The bear bellowed in agony and heaved even harder.

Briggs lost his grip and tumbled to the ground, the impact driving the air from his lungs.

The bear staggered toward him. Briggs tried to force himself to stand, but his legs weren't having it.

Two more strides and the bear was towering over him. It wobbled and fell forward, burying Briggs under a mountain of flesh and fur. But at least it wasn't trying to kill him anymore.

You killed it. Congratulations.

"Thanks. Now how do I get out from under this thing? It must weigh a ton."

I suggest wiggling and pushing.

"You're a huge help."

With no better options, Briggs did as Grimshadow suggested, easing himself out from under the bear an inch at a time. When he finally got free after heaven knew how long, he felt more tired than he ever had in his life.

He managed one step, wobbled, and collapsed on top of his kill.

Resting here is not a good idea.

Briggs didn't doubt that for a moment, but he also found he couldn't move. Hopefully the bear's presence would keep anything else from approaching because Briggs wasn't going anywhere anytime soon.

○

Danny frowned as he collected his and Briggs's plates. Dinner had been excellent, but the kid clearly had things on his mind. Maybe Danny should've found a better way to tell him he was leaving. What that might've been, he had no idea.

He sensed Briggs's life force getting further away by the moment, far further than his nearby room. What was he doing at this hour? It was none of Danny's business, but now his curiosity was piqued. He cleaned the dirty plates with a spell, put them in storage, activated his stealth field, and pursued Briggs.

Outside the tower he spotted the kid making his way across the city toward the forest. Danny shadowed Briggs through the darkened streets. There was no way, even with the demon spirit's magic, for him to sense Danny's presence.

Briggs moved with purpose, navigating the twists and turns without hesitation. Clearly he had a destination in mind. Where that might be Danny was less certain.

Soon the stone streets gave way to dirt as they reached the edge of the forest. Briggs paused at the tree line and drew Grimshadow. The two spoke briefly. Danny could only hear Briggs's side of the conversation, but it sounded like the demon disapproved of whatever he had planned.

That certainly didn't make Danny any less nervous.

Soon enough the conversation ended and Briggs resumed his hunt. Danny made no effort to approach. Whatever was going on, it was really none of his business. Nevertheless, he'd taken a liking to the young beastman and should things go sideways, Danny wouldn't let him get killed.

The hunt continued for a little while before Danny sensed a powerful, corrupt presence. It wasn't a demon exactly, probably a demon-possessed beast of some sort. Whatever it was, Briggs was headed right for it.

Danny leapt into the canopy and watched as a massive bear, its form twisted by corruption, stepped into a clearing in the forest. Briggs stalked closer. Danny found his body tensing as the inevitable conflict got closer.

As soon as he thought it, the fight was on. Briggs landed some slashes that would've killed most men, but the bear shrugged them off like they were nothing.

Eventually he used some sort of short-range teleportation to appear on its back and stab it through the skull. He got thrown off its back and the bear collapsed on top of him. Briggs worked his way out from under it before passing out.

Danny leapt down and checked Briggs for injuries. Aside from some nasty bumps and bruises he seemed unharmed, thank goodness for small favors.

Turning his focus on Grimshadow, Danny projected himself into the demon's awareness. The dark form cowered before him. A strange sight given Grimshadow's size and presence.

"I tried to talk him out of it," the demon said before Danny could ask a question.

"What was the point of this foolishness?" Danny asked.

"He wanted to prove to himself that he was ready to move on to the next stage of rescuing his pack. The bear was a final test. A rite of passage, for lack of a better term."

Danny shook his head. Maybe it was a beastfolk thing. "He fought well."

"Indeed. I wouldn't go so far as to say he's mastered all my abilities, but he can at least use them in battle to good effect. He has become dangerous."

Considering where they were going and what Briggs hoped to accomplish, that could only be a good thing.

Danny willed himself back into his body and looked down at the still-unconscious Briggs. The kid had guts, no doubt. Holy energy infused his body as Danny repaired the relatively minor injuries. Briggs never stirred through the process.

Finally, he returned Grimshadow to the sheath on Briggs's belt, picked the kid up, and put him over his shoulder. Fortunately it wasn't too long of a walk back to Elfhome. On the downside, Danny doubted he'd be getting as early of a start as he originally planned in the morning.

It was a small price to pay for ensuring his friend's wellbeing.

CHAPTER 13

Berend stood impatiently in front of an ornate silver mirror, his red eyes flashing with annoyance as Voss fiddled with the enchanted amulet he'd prepared. The ether crystal Nash had brought back was fitted in the center of a gold frame. The amulet was supposed to hide his demonic features, but so far all it did was make his skin itch.

"How long is this going to take?" Berend asked.

"Until I'm done," Voss said. "Artificing isn't an exact science. It requires patience and constant adjustments. Now be quiet so I can concentrate."

Berend snarled, baring his pointed teeth. He'd never been a vain man, but his new appearance was a problem. Aside from his fighting ability, Berend's main contribution to the team was his ability to collect information. Now that he'd lost his position as assistant guild master and been transformed into a demon, half his value was gone.

Beside him, Voss grumbled an incantation, his fingers tracing arcane symbols in the air. Despite Berend's annoyance, he respected Voss's talent as a wizard. The man would get the amulet working as it was supposed to. And it wasn't like Berend had anything else to do at the moment.

He sighed. Patience had been one of his strong suits back when he was human. Becoming a demon had filled him with restless energy, a constant itch for… something. He wasn't sure what, exactly, but it felt almost like hunger, only not for food. It was unsettling for someone like him to be even somewhat out of control.

"All right, let's try this." Voss dropped the amulet over his neck.

As he watched, his reflection shimmered and started to change, like a mirage in the desert heat. Slowly, his demonic traits melted away, replaced by the ordinary, forgettable features of his former human self. Bald head minus horns, thin but still healthy build, dark, not-at-all-glowing eyes.

"There," Voss said, clearly satisfied with himself. "The illusion will hold as long as you wear the amulet. The ether crystal Nash brought back should be good for six months. I doubt you'll be in the field for that long at this stage of the plan, but keep in mind if you are, your true appearance will return."

"Thanks for the warning. Speaking of Nash, where is he?"

"Sleeping. He ran to the mining camp and back nonstop. That's a lot even for someone as skilled in physical enhancements as him."

Berend grunted and turned away from the mirror. He found looking at his old self uncomfortable. "I need to talk to Zane. Hopefully he's found the merchants."

"He was in the basement temple last I knew," Voss said. He was being remarkably helpful, which Berend mistrusted on principle.

Berend left Voss's workshop and made the short walk to the basement stairs. He stalked down the stone steps to Zane's small temple of Astaroth that was as much a magical workshop as a proper temple.

A closed door waited at the end of a short passage. Berend knocked once before pushing the door open. Inside, Zane was hunched beside a rune circle on the floor, his wiry frame tense with concentration as he drew the precise lines.

A little ways beyond Zane, bloodstains covered the floor. The manacles that had once held the slave sacrifices whose life force paid for Berend's return to the mortal world were empty. The bodies would no doubt be transformed into some sort of undead horror suitable for honoring Astaroth.

Zane looked up as Berend approached, his dark eyes narrowed. "Voss finally got the amulet working I see."

Berend nodded. "Surprised?"

"Not at all. Whatever else you might want to say about Voss, he's a talented wizard."

"What about the merchants? Have you located them?"

"Indeed. As luck would have it, Jerowin is on his way back to Discourt as we speak. He's about a week out from the city. I'll send you back to your place and you can leave from there. He's following the Western Trade Road so finding him shouldn't be a problem."

"If I'm spotted in Discourt, that *will* be a problem," Berend said.

"You're a demon now. Wait until dark, turn invisible, and fly over the wall. Continuing to think like a human will only hold you back."

Berend grimaced. Zane talked like learning to think like a demon was a simple thing. "I'll keep that in mind. Is the portal ready?"

"Nearly. I was putting the finishing touches on when you arrived. Give me a moment and we'll get you on your way."

"A moment" turned out to be most of half an hour. The itching hunger Berend had been fighting came roaring back as he stood waiting. He clenched his jaw and ignored it in hopes the feeling would pass.

It didn't, but Zane finally finished and stood up. "Okay, you're all set. Step into the circle and I'll send you to the marker in your house."

Berend hesitated then asked, "Since the transformation I've been feeling things, a hunger I suppose. What does it mean?"

"It means you're a demon. Demons don't hunger for food or drink, but death. You need to rend some mortal flesh. Make sure you get the feeling out of your system before you meet Jerowin. We don't have so many human allies that we can afford to lose one."

Berend made a fist and relaxed it. Was that what it meant to be a demon? When he made the deal, he hadn't thought much about it beyond knowing it was better than dying.

"Shouldn't be a problem," he said at last. "There are plenty of bums in the poor quarter."

"That's the spirit. Now, into the circle."

Berend stepped into the open center of the rune circle. As soon as he did it started to light up. A moment later the magic swallowed him.

Berend looked down at the twisted, broken body lying in a spreading pool of blood. The dead man's sightless eyes stared up at the night sky, mouth open in a silent scream. At last the hunger that had been gnawing at him since his return from Astaroth's hell was gone, satisfied by the unlucky man's blood. For the first time in days, he felt sated. Calm. Almost like his old self.

It wouldn't last of course, he understood that. He only hoped his demonic appetites wouldn't need satisfying as often as his mortal ones had.

Berend knelt and wiped his blood-slicked hands on the man's tattered shirt. Now that he'd satisfied his immediate needs, it was time to leave Discourt before anyone spotted him. Midnight had come and gone and most of the city was long asleep. The few guards on duty had no magical ability and so no hope of spotting him.

Jerowin was supposed to be a week out from the city which meant he'd need at least two days to reach him even flying.

With no reason to wait, Berend gathered ether and pushed himself into the air. He hovered for a moment, wobbling, as he tried to get a feel for the weightlessness. It was an odd sensation, unlike anything he'd ever felt before.

When he finally steadied, he pictured himself turning invisible. Looking down at himself he saw nothing different. He also didn't feel any different. Had the spell worked? The only way to know for sure was to let someone see him. A stupid idea if ever he'd had one.

Best to just be on his way.

Willing himself skyward, Berend soared out of the slums and into the night sky. He turned west and flew over the wall following the trade road. No alarm was given as he passed between two guard towers. That seemed like a good indication that his invisibility spell was working properly.

Berend soared over the sleeping countryside, the wind whipping past his face as he flew faster than any horse could gallop. At this rate he might not need two days to find Jerowin after all.

Night turned to day but still he didn't slow. He also felt no fatigue or hunger, either for food or blood. He could definitely see the advantages of his new form.

As the afternoon lengthened, he spotted a lone covered wagon guarded by four mercenaries wearing leather armor. He recognized Jerowin's team at once; Berend had been the one to assign the men to guard him after all. Though once they got to Discourt and spoke to Koch, assuming the man survived his encounter with Ronin, a possibility he considered remote, they would likely be looking for new employment.

Berend frowned. None of them knew anything important. As far as they were aware, Avius, in his Carbey persona, was their employer. They certainly knew nothing about Zane and the plan to raise an army of the dead from those slain by the plague.

Should he kill them to be on the safe side? No, unnecessary killing would gain him nothing. Best to make some excuse for how things went to hell and then give Jerowin the new assignment.

Mind made up, Berend flew a mile down the road and landed out of sight before turning visible and beginning the trudge back to Jerowin's wagon.

He heard the creak of the wagon wheels before he saw it. The horses pulling snorted as Berend approached. Despite the magic changing his appearance, the animals still seemed to sense something wasn't right about him.

The guards in front tensed when they spotted him, but quickly relaxed. All of Koch's men had met Berend and knew he was on their side.

"Hold up! Mr. Berend," said the lead guard, a grizzled veteran older than Berend had been when he died. "What are you doing all the way out here in this weather? We would've met you at the estate as planned."

Berend shook his head. "Not a great idea. Some things happened while you were out and the estate is no longer secure. I came to warn you. I don't know if Koch or Avius survived, but I'm not optimistic."

The guards exchanged nervous looks.

Jerowin's head popped out of the flap behind the wagon bench. "What's going... Oh, Berend, I didn't expect to see you out here. Is everything okay?"

"No." Berend repeated what he told the guards. "I don't dare enter the city lest our enemies spot me. I need you to do some legwork for me and report back. Can I count on you?"

Jerowin's throat worked as he tried to swallow. "It sounds dangerous. Perhaps someone else..?"

"There is no one else I can trust to do this. Osbern has already been arrested. I don't know where Albert is at the moment beyond far from here. You're my only option."

"I see..." Jerowin trailed off, clearly not thrilled at the prospect.

"How much did you make selling the cure?" Berend asked.

"A lot. We're completely out of stock."

"You get me the info I need and I'll double your cut and

give all the guards a ten-gold-piece bonus. We'll meet up at the first village north of Discourt in two weeks. Agreed?"

Fear and greed warred on Jerowin's face. Since he was a merchant, greed won. "Very well, I'll ask around, but I'm not doing anything dangerous."

"I don't want you to," Berend said. "If violence is required, I'll handle it. Just find out anything you can about the plague, Carbey, and anything else of interest. I'll see you in two weeks. Oh, if you try to take your earnings and run, I'll hunt you down and cut your eyes out. Clear?"

All the blood drained from Jerowin's face and he nodded.

"Great, good luck." Berend strode off down the road, heading due north. He didn't even know the name of the town where he'd suggested meeting and it didn't matter. Anywhere was good enough. He needed to know what was happening and the sooner the better.

CHAPTER 14

Danny yawned as he studied his map. The sun had risen an hour ago, but he'd sensed nothing from Briggs's room. As expected after his fight last night, the kid was sleeping in. It was annoying, but Danny wasn't in such a big rush that a few hours more or less would be the end of the world. The summoning circle had been there for over a thousand years after all.

He compared the new map to the gazetteer and it became painfully clear that the elf-bloods had no use for exact measurements, at least when it came to maps. They were fussy as hell with the spell casting. As best he could figure, the ether pool he wanted to investigate was a few hundred miles north and a little east. It was the closest to Elfhome and likely served as a power source for the city back in the day. Assuming no blizzards, he should reach the Crystal Mist Mountains in ten days.

Maybe a little longer than that since he planned to visit any villages they passed in the hope of finding out where the beastfolk were taken. Briggs thought they were going in generally the right direction, but that was a far cry from knowing exactly where they were.

There was a knock and he sensed corruption outside the door. It was Riko. He'd spent enough time with the beautiful demon to recognize her unique presence. He put his reading material away and went to the door.

It slid into the floor and he smiled. "What's up?"

"That's what I wanted to ask you. I figured you'd be on the road by now."

"Eager to get rid of me?"

She cocked her head, seeming confused. "Not at all. I only asked because, based on our previous conversation, I thought you planned to depart this morning."

Clearly flirting wasn't something demons were trained in. "I did, but Briggs fought a demonic bear last night and he hasn't woken up yet. He clearly needs the rest and I'm not in that big of a rush. As long as you're here, I wanted to ask if destroying the nearby pool will mess with anything here. It would be rather ungrateful of me if I screwed things up for you as a side effect of my work."

"There will be no problem. All the old wards gave out long ago. The master's temple now serves as the core of the local defenses and the ether pool has no connection to it."

"Great, that's what I was hoping you'd say. And should I need to come back and regroup, that's cool too, right?"

"Of course. The master wishes you to succeed, which means we all wish it as well. However we can help, indirectly, we will."

Danny nodded. "I appreciate it. Never figured I'd end up friends with a demon. The world's full of surprises."

"It certainly is. I remember enough of what it was like to

be human that I've enjoyed our conversations. I will miss you, Daniel."

Danny grinned. He was about to try flirting with her again when he sensed Briggs stir next door. "The kid's awake. I need to finish getting ready."

She offered a little bow. "Best of luck. Good morning."

Riko left and Danny went next door. He knocked and a minute later a bleary-eyed Briggs opened the door. He peered at Danny for a moment. "Grimshadow said you healed me and carried me back. Thanks."

"Glad I could help. Pretty impressive fight against that bear."

"I'm still no match for your power. Grimshadow said I shouldn't compare myself to you." Briggs grinned. "He called you a terrifying human."

"I take that as a compliment from a demon. And he's right. My circumstances are special. You definitely shouldn't compare yourself to me. You're plenty strong enough as you are. Ready to hit the road? I've got cold sausage from breakfast if you're hungry."

"I am. Let me grab Grimshadow and I'll be set."

Danny buckled on his sword and got the food before rejoining Briggs in the hall. He handed the sausage over and Briggs ate as they descended to the first floor. It was strange to think he'd miss a demon-haunted elf-blood city, yet he found himself a bit sad to be going. Danny suspected what he'd really miss was Riko. It was fun talking to someone from Earth, even someone who'd died centuries before he was born.

There was no one waiting to say goodbye when they left the tower. No surprise there. Demons weren't known for their sentimentality.

Danny led the way to the path they used when they arrived.

"We're backtracking?" Briggs asked.

"Yeah. Elfhome is about a hundred miles too far west of the first ether pool. We'll follow the main trade road until we find a side road branching north. We should reach a village eventually where they can tell us about the beastfolk as well as the general lay of the land. I have to think if there's an ether pool under the nearby mountains, it has to have some effect on the area."

"I don't really understand all that magic stuff. I just want to find my pack."

Danny offered a faint chuckle. "I don't understand all of it either. The books I read did more to confirm my ignorance than relieve it. I'm hoping I can figure something out once I see it in person. Listen..."

He hopped over a protruding branch. Danny wasn't sure how best to say what he needed to. There was no easy way to broach the subject. When in doubt direct was probably best.

"Listen," he started again. "If the kidnapped beastfolk have been sold as slaves, it's not going to be a simple thing to free them. Their owners and the local authorities are likely to object, violently."

"The demon bear objected as well," Briggs said. "I will free my pack or die trying. There's no other option. If you don't want to go to war with the local humans, I understand. You've already done a lot for me. I won't ask for more."

Danny sighed. Briggs said exactly what he expected him to. Hopefully, before they reached the first village, he could come up with a plan that was less likely to end up with a lot of people dead.

CHAPTER 15

The stone walls of Discourt cast long shadows over Jerowin and his companions as his guard guided the wagon toward the city gate. He sat on the hard bench to the driver's left. His other three guards marched along beside the wagon. There were no other merchants waiting to enter this early in the morning.

Two armored guards holding halberds stepped into the road to stop him while the remaining ten kept a watchful eye on them. A priest of Branik stood off to one side as he peered closely at the group.

The taller guard held up a mailed fist. "Halt! State your name and business."

How many times had he been told to do that? Jerowin couldn't begin to remember. The ritual was as familiar as putting his boots on in the morning.

"My name is Jerowin and I'm a merchant from Discourt returning after many weeks on the road." He held out his Merchants' Guild membership card which garnered little more than a cursory glance.

The guard looked back at the priest, who nodded. "He's free of disease as are the mercenaries."

The guard shouted, "Raise the portcullis. Welcome back to Discourt. Be sure to report to the Temple of the Goddess to receive your treatment."

"Treatment?" Jerowin asked.

The guard grinned. "The priests have worked out a ritual to make everyone immune to the plague. It's a divine miracle. Some say Mother Ankie received a vision from the Goddess while she was sick. The bulk of the citizens are now immune. In a couple more weeks, we won't even need to check new arrivals."

"Wonderful news," Jerowin said without really meaning it. People with immunity would have no need for a cure potion, which boded ill for business. "Let's go."

The wagon lurched forward, passed under the portcullis and into the streets of Discourt. Jerowin's mind reeled with the unexpected news of the city's miraculous immunity. It was damn lucky for him that he got a full run in before the cure was found. His arrangement wasn't going to be as profitable as he'd hoped, but at least it wouldn't be a complete loss.

"Are we going to the temple?" the driver asked.

"Of course not, we're already immune. I'm going to the Merchants' Guild. You should visit the Mercenaries' Guild and let Captain Koch know we've been contacted by Berend. See if he knows anything about the cure or anything else that's happening in the city."

"What if he's dead?"

"Then find out how he died. I'm sure Berend will want to know. We'll meet up in the morning at the north gate."

"Only if the captain agrees. We answer to him, not you."

"Fair enough. If you want to risk pissing off Berend, be my guest. Frankly, the man scares the hell out of me. I'd no more make an enemy of him than I would hand-feed an Alpha Wolf."

The driver snorted a laugh and turned the wagon off the main street toward the guild district. There was no more conversation and Jerowin focused on the people out and about. They all seemed happy, like a pall had been lifted from the city. No doubt the cure had much to do with the change.

The Merchants' Guild was a huge, sprawling compound with numerous buildings that served various purposes. The driver went to the largest of the bunch, basically a barn where merchants rented space for their horses and wagons.

Jerowin had a modest slot at the rear of the building. The driver guided his wagon into its appointed place and yanked the brake. A pair of stableboys hurried over to tend the horses. Jerowin waved to the mercenaries, who promptly set out for their own guild. Whether they came to meet him in the morning was an open question, one Jerowin couldn't answer so he settled on hoping for the best.

Before heading to the guild office, he collected a heavy pack from the back of the wagon. It held his earnings from this run, the guild's ten percent cut already separated out. It was a fair chunk of coin, but membership had so many benefits he didn't really begrudge them their share.

Jerowin hefted the pack onto his shoulder and strode toward the main guild building. The walk only took moments. Thankfully the bitter cold had come and gone. Soon it would be mud season as the frost went out of the ground. Once it dried, trading season would begin again.

That was every merchant's favorite time of year.

He climbed the steps to the guild office's front door and

pushed it open. The foyer was quiet today. No one did much business this time of year. Jerowin had been one of the few merchants still out on the roads.

A bored-looking clerk sat behind a large wooden desk at the rear of the entry area, idly flipping through a ledger. He glanced up as Jerowin approached. "Can I help you, sir?"

He opened the pack and pulled out a leather pouch that jingled when he set it on the table. "The guild's cut from my last trip."

"Name?" the clerk asked.

"Jerowin."

The young man paged through the ledger, scanning its contents as he went. Finally he stopped and said, "You're not due for an audit this trip. Let me log your payment then you can countersign."

The clerk poured the coins out and start counting.

When he finished, he scribbled in the ledger. "Sign here please." He turned the book around and pointed to a line. Under it was the number one hundred and thirty-six.

That was the correct amount and he signed.

"Know anything about the temple's miracle cure?"

The clerk shrugged. "Not much. Word is, Mother Ankie had a divine revelation and the next day it was announced that a spell had been devised that rendered you immune to the plague. And they were offering it for free. Can you imagine?"

Jerowin could not, in fact, imagine giving away such a thing. They could've made a fortune even if they only charged a silver coin per person. It was completely illogical. But when you were dealing with the temples, you had to expect that sort of thinking.

"You should swing by as soon as you can and get treated,"

the clerk said. "It's painless and only takes about five minutes."

The spell Lord Avius had used on him took about five minutes to complete. Jerowin knew little about magic, but he also didn't believe in coincidences.

"Can you tell me more about the process?"

The clerk grinned. "Nervous?"

"About having a newly devised spell cast on me? You're damn right."

"It's simple. You go into the temple and in the infirmary there are four circles drawn on the floor with all these lines and figures in them. You step into the circle, one of the priests chants a spell, and this white light appears. There's a little tingle, the light vanishes, and they send you on your way. Like I said, five minutes at most and no pain. Now I don't have to worry about getting the plague."

Jerowin nodded. "Thanks for telling me. I'm going home to clean up before I stop by."

He turned on his heel and strode out of the guild office. The process, leaving aside the white light, was identical to Lord Avius's. The temple must've gotten ahold of his notes or something.

All Jerowin knew for sure was that Berend wasn't going to be happy.

○

Captain Darien Koch slammed his fist on the polished hardwood table, the sound echoing through the Mercenaries' Guild's meeting hall. The light from enchanted crystals cast long shadows across the faces of the executive committee members, their expres-

ELFHOME

sions a mix of irritation and boredom. The members hadn't even bothered to dress up. The mixture of leathers and basic tunics displayed their contempt for him as clearly as their faces.

"Damnit, you can't do this to me!" Darien said, his anger barely under control. "I've been a member in good standing for ten years. I deserve a chance to rebuild."

The guild master, an intimidating, heavily muscled warrior despite being in his sixties, sighed. "We've been over this a dozen times. Your company is in shambles. You no longer have the numbers to qualify for membership. It's that simple. If you were only a few dozen short, that would be different, but as it stands your numbers are down by two-thirds. It'll take you months if not years to rebuild. The committee has made its decision."

Darien's mind raced, searching for any argument he hadn't tried, and came up blank. There was no way around the facts, brutal though they were.

He stood and shot them all a hard look. "Fine, but I will rebuild."

The guild master stood as well then came around the table to pat Darien on the back. "We're not your enemy. When you've rebuilt your company, your application to join will be approved, you have my word."

Darien knew the guild master meant well, but the kind words just left him feeling pathetic. "I won't take up any more of your time. Good day, gentlemen."

The guild master returned to his seat and as Darien left the room he heard the discussion shift to other matters, matters that no longer concerned him.

He knew this day was coming. He'd known it since that adventurer, Ronin, decimated his men. He couldn't even hate the man for it. They were both doing their jobs and Ronin ended up being better at his. That was the way things went in the real world. Sometimes you won and often you lost.

Considering what his group had been involved in, he was lucky the temple didn't throw him in prison or worse. Only the fact that he hadn't broken any laws within the walls of Discourt spared him from such an end.

With a little shake of his head, Darien turned and strode down the wood-paneled hall toward the stairs down to the first floor. At least there weren't many people in the guild hall at the moment. Most of the other captains were employed by various wealthy individuals throughout the area and while the leaders might come back to conduct business, the rank and file weren't so fortunate.

His footfalls echoed as he trudged down the steps. At the bottom he was surprised to see four young men waiting. Were they looking to be recruited? Maybe his luck had finally turned around.

They spotted him a moment later and hurried over. The eldest of the group, a corporal judging by his insignia, said, "Captain Koch, we've returned from escorting Jerowin on his trip. The journey was successful and we suffered no losses."

They were his own men, great. Well, at least they were alive to rejoin what remained of the company.

"We also encountered Mr. Berend." Darien's heart lurched. How could they have run into a dead man? The corporal continued, blissfully unaware of Darien's anxiety. "He informed us that our current mission had gone badly and he further requested we gather whatever intel we could before reporting back to him in two weeks at the first village north of here. He offered us a ten-gold-piece bonus."

What should he do now? Darien didn't owe anyone

anything, especially considering how much working for Avius cost him. On the other hand, warning the temple of Berend's return might earn him some goodwill and, with luck, future recruitment.

"You've been misled," Darien said. "Whoever you spoke to, it wasn't Berend, he was killed in an ambush weeks ago. We're going to the Goddess's temple to warn them of the danger. Where's Jerowin? He should come as well."

"We parted company at the Merchants' Guild. I have no idea what he's going to do, but I suspect he'll try to help the fake since he was offered a bigger bonus than us," the corporal said.

"Right, we don't have time to track him down anyway. Let's get out of here. The sooner we pass this off to the temple, the sooner we won't have to worry about it." Darien led the little group out of the guild hall and into the streets of Discourt.

Luckily the guild district wasn't far from the temple district and none of the few people out and about troubled them. Fifteen minutes after leaving the guild hall, the sprawling temple came into view. Darien hadn't planned to be back this soon. Or ever, if he had his way.

He pushed through the always-unlocked front door and into the much warmer entry area. An attractive young woman in a white robe was on duty behind the welcome desk. She looked the five of them over, her smile never wavering.

"Can I help you?" she asked.

"I need to talk to Father Koen. Tell him Captain Koch has news about an old acquaintance of Lord Carbey's. He'll be eager to speak with me." Darien made sure to keep the information vague since he had no idea what the higher-ups might've shared with the lower-ranking priests.

"Father Koen has been terribly busy. Are you su—"

"I'm sure. It's a matter of life and death. Please tell him."

She hesitated for another moment then said, "Okay, wait here."

When the priestess had hurried into the infirmary the corporal asked, "Do you know Father Koen, sir? He's a fairly high-ranking member of the priesthood if I recall correctly."

"The second highest in fact," Darien said. "We met briefly once immediately after the chaos at the estate. He should be able to help us with Berend or whatever you ran into."

Ten minutes later Father Koen came shuffling into the entry area by himself. He looked like hell and Darien almost felt bad about bothering him. Almost.

"This better be important, Captain," Father Koen said.

"My men ran into Berend on their way back to the city. He asked them to spy on Discourt and report back in two weeks. Impressive for a dead man, wouldn't you say?"

"Not another word," Father Koen said. "Follow me."

He led Darien and his men deeper into the temple, through the chapel, and into the halls beyond. Eventually they ended up at an empty meeting room not much different from the one where his career as a guild captain ended.

"Stay here. I need to get a couple more people." With that rather brusque order, Father Koen left them to their own devices.

"What's going on, sir?" the corporal asked.

"Nothing good, you can be sure of that. For simplicity's sake, it would be best if you kept quiet unless asked a question. I have no doubt the people coming will have plenty. Be honest. We have nothing to hide and have done nothing wrong. Understand?"

"Yes, sir."

Father Koen returned half a minute later and he had prestigious company in the form of Mother Ankie and Avius. The wizard had discarded his disguise of Lord Carbey, for the moment at least.

"Koch," Avius said. "Tell me everything."

Darien did so, repeating all that the soldiers had told him. When he finished, they were asked to repeat the story in their own words.

At the end Avius nodded. "They're telling the truth. I didn't imagine Berend would find a way back so quickly. How unfortunate. It will be necessary to kill him a second time."

"What is he?" Mother Ankie asked. She looked much stronger than the last time Darien saw her.

"A demon of some sort," Avius said. "I couldn't say exactly what variety without getting a closer look and it doesn't matter anyways. All demons need killing. At least he was thoughtful enough to tell us where to find him."

"We can't spare anyone and our healers aren't trained for fighting demons," Father Koen said.

"I'll contact the temple of Branik," Mother Ankie said. "They have a special team of knights to handle this sort of thing. Thank you, Captain, for bringing this news to us so quickly."

"Of course," Darien said. "I might be a sell-sword, but I don't want demons running around any more than you do. Is there anything else?"

"Actually," Father Koen said. "It would be helpful if you

could find the merchant and make sure he doesn't alert Berend. It would be a paid job."

Darien grinned. "I'm your man. Koch's Raiders are at the temple's service. Now let's talk price."

Darien barely restrained himself from rubbing his hands together. If they played this right, a long-term job with the temple might be in the cards. He wouldn't even need to rebuild the company if that happened.

Who would've guessed a simple good deed could lead to something so positive?

CHAPTER 16

Danny stood in a grove of trees, studying a village nestled in the valley below. The houses had cedar roofs and smoke trickled out of chimneys. The people were moving around seemingly undaunted by the muddy street. The village was surrounded by dormant fields for miles in every direction. The farms were broken only by the hard-packed road running through them. Everything looked as he expected save one thing.

"Where are the slaves?" Briggs asked.

"Good question. Maybe the people of this village don't use them. Why don't you wait here while I take a look around?"

"If my mother or the others are here, I have to know."

"If there are any beastfolk slaves, I'll tell you, I promise. For now, let me go in alone. The locals won't give a visiting adventurer a second look. Considering the recent tension, a beastman might not be treated so well. It won't take more than a couple hours."

Briggs didn't look thrilled, but he finally nodded.

Danny activated his stealth field, shimmering out of visibility, and started down the hill. Once he reached the road, he ended the spell and approached openly. He sensed many life forces, all human as far as he could tell.

A couple guards were on duty at a makeshift gate that blocked the road. They didn't even have armor and their spears were crude to say the least. A less intimidating duo Danny could hardly imagine.

"Halt and state your business," the right-hand guard said.

"I'm Ronin, an adventurer passing through on my way to the Crystal Mist Mountains. I was hoping to buy some supplies. I'm not from the area so any information about the local dangers would be welcome."

"Let's see your guild card," the same guard said.

Danny handed it over. He had serious doubts that a village guard would be able to tell the difference between a real guild card and a fake, but if it made him feel better about letting Danny in, that was fine.

After a few seconds of intense staring the guard handed it back. "Okay. Welcome to Snowy Valley. If you need a place to stay, we have a tavern that also lets rooms. Far as I know they're both vacant."

Danny smiled at the pleasantly warm welcome. "Much obliged, sir. On another note, I heard from an acquaintance of mine that there were slave auctions in this area. I've never been to one, but I admit I'm curious."

The guard shook his head. "Nasty business. It might be legal, but most people dislike the practice. We keep no slaves here. They're more common in the towns around Crystal Lake. Processing fish, cutting timber, and mining are all hard jobs and the men who own the businesses are always looking for cheap help. Doesn't come much cheaper than a slave."

"Thanks. Think I'll visit that tavern you mentioned and get a drink. Weeks on the road make a man thirsty."

The guard laughed. "Standing guard has the same effect. Maybe we can share a mug when my shift is over."

"I look forward to it."

The silent guard lifted the crooked sapling that served as a gate out of the way and Danny strode through. There was no priest to check him for plague and the guards were relaxed. Maybe the disease hadn't made it this far. Seemed unlikely to Danny, but he wouldn't complain about his good luck.

The village's lone street ran straight through the village. The people out and about doing whatever errands stared at him as he passed. As with most small villages, an outsider was both a curiosity and a source of entertainment. If he hung around long enough there would no doubt be many questions asked at the tavern.

Speaking of, he spotted the tavern a moment later. It was the only two-story building in the village, with a weathered sign depicting a frothing mug of ale swinging above the door. Danny pushed inside, greeted by the warmth of a crackling hearth and the low murmur of conversation.

A few patrons glanced up as he entered, but most remained focused on their drinks and companions. Danny approached the bar where a balding, heavyset man was wiping down mugs with a wet rag.

"What'll it be?" The barkeeper favored Danny with a serious looking over. There was nothing mean or aggressive in the man's gaze, just curiosity, same as everyone else.

"Ale, thanks." Danny slapped a gold coin on the bar. "And information."

The barkeeper looked from Danny to the coin and back

before shrugging and snatching it off the bar. He poured the drink and set a mug in front of Danny.

"We don't get much news out here, but ask away, you certainly paid well enough for it."

Danny took a long swig of the ale, savoring the sweet, malty taste. It was by far the best drink he'd had since arriving on Valindor. Whatever the brewmasters were doing, he approved.

He set the mug down. "I'm looking for some friends of mine. They were taken by slavers a few weeks back. Heard they might've been brought this way."

The barkeeper's expression darkened. He glanced around furtively before speaking in a low voice. "Slavers pass through these parts, but they never bother Snowy Valley. Not sure why. Our guards couldn't stop a determined attack. Maybe we don't look like we'd make good merchandise. Anyway, those slaves are headed straight for Crystal Lake."

"The gate guard mentioned Crystal Lake. What can you tell me about the area?"

"It's the biggest lake around here. Everything flows into it. It's loaded with fish. Three big merchant companies control access. Between them they have a couple hundred slaves catching and processing everything from salmon to eels. Lot of gold being made. But the fishing's nothing compared to the ether crystal mine. That's where you'll find the bulk of the slaves and the bulk of the gold."

"What are ether crystals?" Danny hadn't heard of them before.

"I don't know anything specific, but they're supposed to be useful for making magic items. How it works I couldn't tell you." The barkeeper made a vague gesture at the tavern. "Magic's a little outside my area of expertise."

Danny chuckled. "I'm an arcane knight and I've never even heard of them, so you're one up on me. Thanks for the drink."

He polished off his ale and started to turn for the door.

"It's getting late. Want a room for the night? I'll give you a deal."

"I appreciate the offer, but we've got a few more hours of daylight and I want to reach the lake as soon as possible. If you're right and my friends ended up at the mine, any delay might cost them."

The barkeeper glanced around and lowered his voice. "Best watch what you say. The closer you get to the lake, the less understanding people get about the fate of slaves."

"I'll take that to heart. Good evening." Danny turned and strode out of the tavern.

If the slaves were all being held in a relatively small area, freeing them and escaping might not be as difficult as he feared. And if the ether crystals weren't related to the ether pool under the mountains he'd eat his sword.

Danny walked through the town and exited on the opposite side. That was enough to let him confirm the absence of any beastfolk. At a minimum, Briggs's pack mates weren't here and he'd sensed no lie from the barkeeper or the guard he spoke with. The village really did seem to have no use for slaves.

Twenty minutes later he reached the trees where he left Briggs.

"Did you find them?" The eager question came the instant Danny arrived.

Danny shook his head. "There are no beastfolk in the village and no slaves of any sort. But I did pick up a lead."

Briggs perked up. "What is it?"

Danny repeated what the barkeeper had told him. "Odds are they're at the mine. Beastfolk are stronger than humans. Mining would be a perfect job for them. At a minimum it's a place to start."

Briggs grinned. "Then what are we waiting for?"

"Nothing. Let's go."

CHAPTER 17

Darien strode into the Merchants' Guild and made a quick survey of the nearly empty hall. He'd expected to find the place crawling with merchants planning their spring trade runs. Maybe it was still too early. He had little enough to do with merchants as a rule and had no idea about their schedules. For now, he needed to focus on finding Jerowin.

A single, youthful clerk manned the desk at the rear of the hall. He watched Darien march his way, a little frown creasing his lips as he smoothed his dark-gray tunic.

"Can I help you, sir?" the clerk asked when Darien stopped in front of him.

"I'm looking for Jerowin. My men guarded him during his last run and there are a couple matters we need to discuss. I had hoped to catch him here, but it seems my luck is running as sour as usual."

"Who are you, sir?"

"Darien Koch, captain in the Mercenaries' Guild." Technically former captain but he doubted word had gotten around yet.

"Ah, Captain Koch, of course. The guild extends its thanks for the fine work your men did looking after one of our members. Jerowin didn't make an error on his payment, did he?"

"Nothing so serious. Just a couple minor technical details on his next run we need to work out now that a plague immunity spell has been found."

"Right, Jerowin asked me about that. He seemed a bit upset. Hardly surprising given his merchandise on his last run."

"I'm sure." Darien had been nearly certain Jerowin would've heard about the cure spell given how it was the biggest item of discussion in the city, but this confirmed it. "Do you know where he went?"

"Home, I assume. Most merchants are eager to sleep in their own bed and enjoy a home-cooked meal after months on the road. Do you have his address?"

Darien smiled. "I don't."

"One moment." The clerk reached under the counter and pulled out a ledger. He flipped through the pages and stabbed a particular entry with his index finger. "Here we are. Eighty-seven Bronze Street in the merchant district. Barely. Given his take on the last run I wonder if he'll be looking to upgrade."

Darien couldn't have cared less about Jerowin's living arrangements. "Thanks. I'll be on my way."

He nodded to the clerk, turned on his heel, and marched back out of the guild. He had just reached the street when his men came running. Darien had sent them to search the immediate area with little hope of them finding anything.

Since the four men were on their own, it seemed his lack of optimism had been warranted.

"No luck?" he asked.

"Not a peep, sir," Corporal Lawler said.

"I struck out at the guild as well, but I did get his home address. Let's go."

Darien's men fell in behind him as he strode toward Bronze Street. It was strange to find people out and about, smiling and at ease. You'd never guess to look at them that a lethal plague had been the talk of the city only weeks ago. The mood was certainly an improvement, but it would take some getting used to.

They approached Jerowin's residence, a modest two-story stone house with a tiled roof. It was so small it barely qualified for this address and wouldn't even be an outbuilding at the bigger mansions.

Darien paused, studying the building for any signs of life. The curtains were drawn, and no smoke rose from the chimney. That couldn't be a good sign. It was chill enough that no one would be home without a fire.

He sighed, climbed the three steps up to the door, and rapped his knuckles against the wood. No response, confirming his worries. The door rattled when he tried it. Locked of course.

"What now, sir?" Lawler asked.

"Now we go back to the temple and tell them they'd best hurry if they want to find Berend before Jerowin warns him."

Berend stepped out of New Stand's lone tavern into the harsh morning sunlight, squinting against the glare. He'd been holed up in this dingy backwater town for over a week, waiting impatiently for his informants to arrive. They weren't even due for another five days and his lack of patience annoyed him no end.

Killing a pair of farmers two days ago helped a bit, but he was already getting twitchy. Being a demon was a bigger challenge than he'd expected.

He flexed his hand, the talons hidden by an illusion of the man he used to be. The power more than made up for any inconvenience. He'd torn those men apart as easily as a wolf might a rabbit. It was intoxicating.

He shaded his eyes. A lone rider was approaching down the dirt road into town. As the rider drew closer, Berend's eyes widened in surprise. It was Jerowin. Alone.

Where were the mercenaries and what was Jerowin doing here so early? The answers, he feared, wouldn't please him.

Jerowin reined in his horse in front of the tavern and dismounted beside Berend. He flicked the reins around the hitching post and said, "I have some unfortunate news."

"Let's go inside and have a drink. You look like you could use one."

Jerowin laughed. "Maybe more than one."

They went inside and Berend guided the merchant to a corner table before waving to the tavern's lone serving girl. She had to be over forty and looked like she'd lived those years hard if the jaundiced eyes and deep wrinkles were any indication.

"What can I get you?" she asked.

"Brandy if you have some," Jerowin said. "And a bowl of whatever's cooking in the back."

The woman's gaze shifted to Berend. "For you?"

He hadn't needed to eat since coming back from Hell and just shook his head.

She went to the kitchen and Berend asked, "Where are the mercenaries?"

"We parted company at the guild and I haven't seen them since. I assume they found something else to do. My news wouldn't wait so I rode out right away."

"Tell me."

Jerowin took a breath to speak but before he could the server returned carrying a steaming bowl and a small glass. She set them in front of him with a quick, "Here you go." Then she was gone again.

"You were saying," Berend said.

"The temple is offering to make people immune to the plague. They've already done most of Discourt. I spoke to someone at the guild and the process sounds exactly the same as what Avius did to me. What are the odds they came up with the exact same answer to the problem?"

"Damn little." Berend ground his teeth. "I'll wager gold to copper Ronin captured Avius and forced him to talk."

"What are we going to do? Once the roads clear I was planning to collect another load of cure potions and set out. That's not going to work very well if immunity is being offered for free."

Berend didn't bother pointing out that they had no more cure potions for him to sell. Zane wasn't going to be pleased. He might have to activate the transformation ritual early and hope for the best. Either way, it was time for Berend to get back. Just as soon as he tied up a few loose ends.

Jerowin was devouring his soup, seeming completely unaware of his pending death.

Berend was about to rip his head off when he heard the clatter of many hooves outside. What the hell now?

He stood and went to the window. Outside the tavern, a dozen knights were dismounting, their armor covered by light-gray tabards featuring the inverted sword.

Berend had seen Branik's elite knights in Discourt many times and refused to believe they were just passing through. "You led them to me."

"Led who to you?" Jerowin asked around a mouthful of soup.

No one could feign a stare that blank. But if Jerowin hadn't led the knights to him, how did they end up here?

The answer, obviously, was the mercenaries. They must've talked to someone, someone who knew Berend had been killed. It wouldn't be hard for a priest to figure out what his return to the land of the living likely meant.

Looked like he was in for a fight. A slow smile spread across his face. Giving his new powers a proper test wouldn't be the worst thing. Though twelve against one was a bit worse odds than he would've preferred.

"What's going on?" Jerowin asked.

Berend lashed out, ripping the merchant's throat open. The serving girl screamed, but he ignored both her and the bleeding corpse. There would be no further need for the merchant given the current state of the plague.

He stood and glanced out the window again. The knights were approaching the tavern door and would enter soon. He needed to be ready. He debated going out to meet them, but it was probably better to fight in the doorway so they couldn't come at him all at once.

Berend took a steadying breath, a leftover reaction from

when he still needed to breathe, and positioned himself beside the door.

And not a moment too soon.

The first knight stepped inside, his sword drawn and ready. "Show yourself, demon!"

Berend obliged.

With inhuman speed, he lunged at the knight, knocking the sword aside and sinking his talons into the man's throat. A hard yank sent blood spraying across the tavern floor, splattering against walls in vivid crimson streaks.

The rest of the knights rushed in shouting for vengeance.

Berend grinned, almost intoxicated by the aroma of blood filling the air as the knight crumpled to the ground, his life extinguished.

The others surged forward, swords glinting.

Berend was already moving. He twisted sideways, avoiding a thrust aimed at his midsection. The knight's sword crackled with holy energy.

Someone shouted, "Surround him! Don't let the demon escape!"

Berend had no intention of escaping. He was going to kill them all.

He lashed out again, claws outstretched as he ripped into another knight's armor.

His target raised his sword in time to turn the blow aside. Berend hissed when the holy magic burned his hand. It was the first pain he'd felt since being reborn and he didn't like it at all.

He spun and struck a backhanded blow that sent the knight flying. Metal crunched as he slammed into the wall.

No time to savor his success. Half a dozen knights had

made it through the door and they were moving to encircle him.

Perhaps he'd been a bit over optimistic in thinking he could kill them all on his own. Escape struck him as a fine idea and the sooner the better.

He dashed toward the bar. A shoulder tackle sent a knight sprawling.

Pain burned down his back as one of the knights struck a glancing blow with his enchanted sword.

Berend grabbed a stool and hurled it at an approaching knight with enough force to crush the man's helmet.

He leapt over the bar and smashed through the door into the kitchen, enraged knights right on his heels.

"After him!" someone shouted. "There's no back door. We've got the bastard now!"

Idiots. Did they think he needed a door to get outside?

He ignored the trembling serving girl and a man he assumed was the cook and ran straight for the rear wall. A wave of darkness rushed ahead of him. It rotted the timbers and when he hit them he burst through and out into the cold afternoon air.

As soon as he was clear, Berend leapt into the air and flew north, back to the fortress. He needed to let Zane and the others know their efforts had fallen apart. Hopefully they had a backup plan because he had no doubt the knights would be doing all they could to hunt him down now that they knew he'd returned.

CHAPTER 18

Danny and Briggs trudged along the hard dirt road that led to Crystal Lake. They'd left the Western Trade Road behind days ago. Danny had lost track of exactly how many, but they had to be getting close. He had no evidence of that, but they'd been making good time so hopefully today or tomorrow they'd spot the lake.

He took a deep breath and grimaced. There was a hint of something… rotten in the air. Not a battlefield, he knew that smell all too well. No, this was something else.

"Can you smell that?" he asked.

"I've been smelling it for hours," Briggs said. "Reminds me of an antelope that died and stayed out in the sun too long."

Danny couldn't comment on the accuracy of the observation, having never smelled a rotten antelope, but it sounded right.

The sun hung low on the horizon as they rounded a sharp bend in the road. Ahead of them, Crystal Lake gleamed in the distance. The beauty of the lake combined with the picturesque buildings surrounding it brought him up short.

"Wow. Now that's a view."

"Finally," Briggs said. "Now we can find and free my pack."

"I've got an idea about how to do that, but I'm not sure you'll like it."

"Tell me."

"I thought I'd take you into the nearest town and pretend you're a slave I want to sell to the mine. Hopefully someone will direct us to it. Once we know where to look, sneaking in and confirming your pack's presence will be easy. Freeing them and escaping will be less easy, but if we can skirt the settlements, it should be possible."

"I hate the idea of pretending to be a slave. Can't you just go in on your own and ask? You had no trouble at the last village."

Danny frowned. "If it bothers you that much, I can try. The mine is supposed to sell ether crystals. I could pose as a buyer."

"I like that better. I've gotten used to waiting outside of town for you to return. If I saw a beastfolk slave, even one not of my pack, I fear I might not be able to control myself."

"Fair enough. I should be able to make it to the nearest village before dark. Let's backtrack and find you a good campsite."

"I'm not a kid. I'll find a place on my own."

Danny swallowed a sigh. "Okay. I'll get a room in town and meet up with you in the morning."

They parted ways and Danny hurried toward the distant town. Dusk was settling over the place when he reached the palisade that surrounded it on three sides. There was a single gate just big enough to allow one wagon at a time to pass through, guarded by a squad of six soldiers dressed in leather armor and carrying spears. They looked reasonably professional. What was lacking was a priest to check for sick people. Once again it appeared he'd moved beyond the plague's range. That came as a surprise and a relief.

He debated turning invisible and leaping the wall, but saw no reason to since he'd done nothing wrong.

Danny marched up to the gate and paused when one of the guards raised a gauntleted hand.

"Name and purpose of your visit?" The old reliable questions.

"I'm Ronin, a traveling adventurer. I was hoping to buy some ether crystals to trade as I go."

"You might find a few here," the guard said. "But you'll need to go to the other side of the lake if you're looking to buy in bulk. Crystal Veil Trading has a monopoly on ether crystals, but they still offer discounts if you buy a large quantity."

"Good to know," Danny said. "I'm impressed you're so informed."

"Are you kidding? Do you have any idea how many merchants pass through this gate? All I hear day in and day out are stories about deals, who's dealing with whom, you name it and some merchant is blabbing about it."

Danny laughed at the man's exasperated expression. "That's certainly different from where I'm from. Our merchants are very tight-lipped about their business. They think everyone's looking to steal a copper they might get for themselves."

"Consider yourself lucky. Go on through."

"As long as you're offering information, could you recommend a good inn, preferably away from the smell of rotting fish?"

Now it was the guard's turn to laugh. "There's nowhere in Fishkill you can escape the stink. Take a few deep breaths and you'll eventually burn out your sense of smell so you no longer notice. As for inns, your best bet is The Tipsy Trout. Through the gate, take a left, and keep going until you see a sign with a fish jumping out of a mug. That's the place."

"Thanks." Danny left the guards behind before they decided to ask for an entry fee. It was strange they didn't. All the towns he'd visited with professional guards asked for one. He assumed it was to cover the cost of the soldiers.

He shrugged and turned left. How hard could it be to find a sign with a fish and a mug?

Danny made his way down the main street, the light getting dimmer with each stride, keeping his eyes peeled for the right sign. There was no one out and about, which surprised him. He doubted anyone was still working at this hour.

At last, Danny spotted The Tipsy Trout. The sign, a remarkable carving that really did look like a trout jumping out of a foaming mug of ale, swung back and forth in the evening breeze, the chain squeaking as it did.

The tavern itself had seen better days. The weathered exterior was stripped down to bare boards and the two windows were the cheapest, cloudiest glass Danny had ever seen. Hopefully the inside was better than the outside.

He pushed open the heavy door and stepped inside. The common room was dimly lit by a large open fire pit that filled the air with smoke and the pleasant scent of burning cedar. It was a vast improvement over the smell outside. Half a dozen tables held about twenty rough-looking men nursing their drinks and shoveling in some kind of cream soup. It didn't look especially appetizing. Hopefully it wasn't the only thing on the menu.

The men eyed Danny as he approached the bar but no one made a move to trouble him. Probably just curious about the new face. Danny was used to getting looked at and paid them no mind.

At the bar he caught the eye of the barkeep, a burly man with a thick black beard streaked with gray. He was busy rearranging the inn's meager collection of alcohol.

When he finally finished, he asked, "What'll it be?"

"A room for the night, a hot meal that's not whatever everyone else is eating, and any information you might have on ether crystals," Danny said, keeping his voice low.

"How's fried trout sound?"

"Delicious."

"Good, because that's the only other thing we have. A room's no problem, I have four available. As for ether crystals, you'll need to talk to someone from Crystal Veil Trading. They've got a monopoly."

"I was thinking I might go right to the mine and cut out the middle man. Or do they own that too?"

The barman shrugged his broad shoulders. "Beats me. A few people have gone looking for it over the years. None of them came back breathing. Unless you're invited by a Veil merchant or you're a beastfolk slave, I'd stay away from the mountains. Find a seat. I'll fix your food."

Danny ambled over to the nearest table and settled in. Whoever was running the mine must have some serious security. That said, unless there were a bunch of high-level demons guarding the place, he was pretty sure he could manage. On the plus side, it sounded like everyone was afraid of the place. If they could free the slaves, it would probably be a while until anyone came looking for them.

All things considered, the situation could've been worse. He'd collect Briggs in the morning and start scouting the mountains. Finding the mine should be easy enough. Dealing with the guards, well, if they wanted to be reasonable, that was fine with Danny. If not, he wouldn't feel bad about killing evil men to free good ones.

◯

Briggs sat on an old stump and sighed. The little fire he'd built crackled and popped, sending sparks into the night air. It was chilly despite the fire, but beast-folk weren't bothered by extreme temperatures the same way humans were.

He shouldn't have gotten annoyed with Ronin, but sometimes his human friend treated him like he was just a dumb little kid. Briggs had survived on his own weeks after his escape; he could camp out for a night without getting into trouble.

They were so close now the minutes dragged by. Hopefully they'd find his mother tomorrow. And the rest of the pack of course, but it was her Briggs really wanted to see. And he would, no matter what he had to do.

His stomach growled and Briggs pulled out a strip of jerky. Though he could manage on his own, Ronin's cooking was far better than cold, dry meat. Maybe he was getting soft.

You're not the only one who's hungry. You haven't killed anything in weeks.

"Didn't you spend years with nothing to eat before I became your bearer?" Briggs asked.

Yes, but that doesn't make it enjoyable.

One thing that had struck Briggs about Grimshadow was, despite the demon's considerable power, he liked to complain about his hunger. That seemed strange considering he was only a spirit in a dagger. He didn't even have a stomach to fill.

Rustling from the trees that screened him from the road brought Briggs out of his thoughts. Someone... He cocked his head and listened hard. No, multiple people, were headed his way.

Four people, all humans. Grimshadow's confirmation put Briggs on full alert. Around here, humans and beastfolk weren't on the best terms.

Briggs slid Grimshadow from his sheath and put the dagger behind his back out of sight. The smell of unwashed bodies caught his attention a moment before the men entered his campsite.

They were a rough-looking bunch. Tattered clothes, unshaven faces, weary, bitter looks in their eyes. Bandits or slavers probably. Either way, bad news.

Not necessarily. At least I'll get something to eat.

Briggs ignored the comment and stood to greet his unwelcome visitors. The biggest of the lot, a burly man with a scar down his cheek, stepped forward. "Didn't expect to find a beastfolk in these parts. At least not one without a collar. You a runaway, boy?"

"No, I'm passing through and not looking for company. You'd best find your own campsite."

"But this is a nice spot," the big man said. "Plenty of room for all of us. We'll just tie you up and after a good night's sleep, we'll run you into town and make sure you're not a runaway. If you're telling the truth, there won't be any trouble."

A couple of the other men snickered.

"I'm going nowhere with you and if you think I'm going to let you tie me up, think again. If you and your friends walk away right now, there won't be any trouble."

This comment brought full-throated laughs from the men.

"Someone hand me a rope and we'll find out how tough this brat is." One of the men handed their leader a coil of heavy rope and he took a step closer to Briggs.

When he was a stride away, Briggs whipped Grimshadow around and drove the curved blade up and into the man's throat. A sideways yank all but severed his head.

The rapidly bleeding corpse dropped to the dirt.

Briggs fell into a crouch. "Who wants to try and tie me up next?"

The remaining men stared at their leader's body. Blood pooled around him, the stink of it even worse than the humans' unwashed bodies.

You can't let them go. If you do, they'll return with so many humans you'll have no chance of beating them.

"You're dead, boy!" said a short, broad man who looked like he had dwarf ancestry. He gripped a heavy club in both hands. The others pulled thick-bladed knives and edged closer.

He didn't wait for them to rush him.

Briggs leapt at the rightmost human, his speed and strength enhanced by Grimshadow's magic. The demon's hunger for life force drove him on.

He evaded a clumsy thrust and slashed the man's throat as he passed.

That was two down.

The man with the club swung wildly at Briggs's head.

He ducked under the clumsy attack, darted in, and slashed with Grimshadow, opening the attacker's belly. Steaming entrails spilled out as the man crumpled.

Briggs spun to face the final attacker. The man's knife trembled in his hand.

He threw the knife aside. "I'll leave, please, just don't kill me."

Briggs took a step closer and the human took one back. "Would you have given me the same consideration if our positions were reversed?"

"I'm begging here. Please."

You know what he'll do if you let him go.

Grimshadow was right. He knew it, but he didn't have to like it. Killing in the heat of battle was one thing but murdering this pathetic excuse for a man would get him nowhere.

With no conscious thought on his part, Briggs lunged, slashing hard and cutting the final man's throat.

The human collapsed, a look of disbelief twisting his face.

"You made me do that." Briggs stared at the dagger.

I didn't make you do anything you didn't want to do. Your hesitation was pitiful. You won't be able to complete your mission with such weak determination.

"We practically murdered him. However necessary it might've been, it was also wrong."

Are you worried about your soul, at this late date? You've already made a pact with a demon. Rest assured, your fate is the master's hell and nothing else you might do between now and when he claims your soul will change that. Best make peace with reality. Hesitate again and you'll be visiting Black City far sooner than you might like.

"Stop reading my thoughts." Briggs jammed Grimshadow back into his sheath and kicked one of the dead men over onto the fire, snuffing it out.

I live in your mind as much as in the dagger. I can no more stop reading your thoughts than I can stop being a demon. Thank you for the fine meal by the way. Their life force was delicious.

Briggs grimaced and stalked out into the night. He needed to find a new campsite. As he walked he tried his best to ignore Grimshadow's mocking laughter ringing in his head.

CHAPTER 19

At his top flying speed Berend needed only a couple of days to reach the team's fortress. The shallow cut in his back had already healed, but the burning pain of the holy sword's touch was seared into his memory. If he was going to have to fight more of the holy warriors, a possibility he considered almost certain, getting a proper suit of armor and a weapon better than his claws was a priority.

Of course, that meant relying on Voss, not a prospect that excited him. Not because he thought the wizard less than competent so much as he disliked relying on anyone other than himself. Doing so was just asking for trouble.

Berend landed in the courtyard and made his way toward the dark stone keep. The early morning was silent. The group kept no living servants, only Zane's and Voss's demonic familiars as well as some lesser undead. It was easier that way since there was no need to worry about someone speaking out of turn, taking time off, or complaining. Any one of which was likely to result in a living servant making a speedy transition to undeath.

Berend entered the keep, his footsteps echoing through the empty halls. He made his way to the stairs down to Zane's private temple. He didn't know if the priest would be there, but it was as good a place to start his search as any. He wasn't going to be thrilled with the news of the plague cure, but hopefully Astaroth would have some way to keep the situation from becoming a total loss.

Berend descended the steps into the depths of the keep. The darkness proved no impediment to his demon eyes. Step by step the air grew cooler and more welcoming. It felt like the darkness was embracing him, welcoming him home.

At the bottom of the steps, the flickering light of torches burning with blood-red, magical light cast eerie shadows on the walls.

He reached the heavy wooden door to Zane's private temple slash workshop and pushed it open. The man himself stood in front of the altar, his pale hands clasped in prayer. A fresh corpse rested on the altar and corrupted ether flowed into it. His murmured incantation continued until red lights appeared in the corpse's eyes and it sat up.

Zane unclasped his hands and turned to face Berend. "I didn't expect you back so soon. I take it the news is less than encouraging."

"You take it correctly." Berend told him everything that happened. "I figure the temple either found something useful in Avius's notes or somehow brought the wizard under their control. Nothing else makes sense."

Berend knew Zane well enough to recognize his tightly controlled fury. Only the narrowed eyes and clenched jaw gave it away and they were so subtle anyone else wouldn't have noticed.

"Lord Astaroth will not be pleased by this outcome."

"Can't you do something? Change the plague again so the immunity no longer applies?"

"If only it were that simple. Changing it the first time was possible by piggybacking off Avius's work. My magic isn't nearly powerful enough to change something over such a large area. No, I fear our best option is to raise what forces we can, collect them, and fall back to the main temple. Hundreds of undead aren't as good as thousands, but they aren't nothing. We should be able to carve out a nice little kingdom of the dead. Over time we'll expand. The process will not be speedy, but one thing followers of the Lord of the Undead have in abundance is time."

Berend wasn't thrilled about Zane's answer, but he also wasn't surprised. "How long will it take?"

"I need ten large ether crystals, then I have to corrupt them. Probably a month at least. I'll send Nash for the crystals at once."

"I'm sure he'll be delighted, knowing how much he loves visiting Vulmar. Unless there's something else, I need to talk to Voss about some armor and a proper weapon."

"I don't know about armor," Zane said. "But I have a sword here I think might suit you."

He walked into the darkest part of the room, where the shadows were so deep even Berend's demon eyes couldn't pierce them, and a moment later came back with a straight-bladed sword made of inky black metal in one hand and a black leather sheath in the other.

"Hell-forged black iron. Only a demon can wield it properly. I summoned it from Astaroth's hell not long after your return. Had I known what you'd encounter, I would've had you wait to check in with Jerowin."

Berend took the weapon and gave it a couple of practice

swings. It felt right in his hand, like it was made to be there, which in a way it sort of was. He knew a little about Hell-forged iron. A normal human trying to wield it would likely lose a hand from its inherent corruption. That same energy made a demon stronger.

"This will do nicely. Perhaps I should go back and repay those knights for the wound they gave me."

Zane shook his head. "Don't waste your time. There will be plenty of battles to come, no need to go looking for one."

Berend laughed. "I'm a demon now. All I think about is killing."

"That is a failing of your kind. Best learn to master it lest it lead you to destruction. Unlike the soft power of Heaven, to wield Hell's power effectively requires strength of will and discipline. Since you've always had plenty of both, I'm sure you'll figure it out."

"I appreciate your vote of confidence," Berend said without really meaning it. "Where is Voss anyway?"

"In the fortress somewhere. Beyond that I haven't the slightest idea. Try his lab or the library."

Berend grunted and marched out of the temple, buckling on his new sword as he went. He'd try the library first. It was on the way and would only take a minute to check.

He was halfway there when he sensed an approaching life force. A moment later Nash stepped into the corridor. The blind swordsman's empty gaze had never bothered Berend, though he knew it unsettled weaker men.

"Nash."

"Berend. Zane summoned me. Do you know what he wants?"

"Ten large ether crystals."

Nash grimaced. "I had hoped to avoid Vulmar for the rest of my life. Can't you do it?"

"I could, but I wouldn't want to deprive you of the opportunity to do something for the cause."

"Generous of you. I'd blame your cruelty on the transformation, but you were just as bad when you were alive."

Berend grinned, his pointed teeth flashing in the weak light. "Have fun, Nash."

Nash shot him a rude gesture and strode on. Nothing like a little levity after a bad day. Now back to the business at hand. Two turns later he reached the library door.

Berend pushed open the heavy door and stepped through. The drifting dust made the air look almost misty. You wouldn't think a couple hundred books would be enough to make that much dust, but then again undead and demons didn't make for the best housekeepers.

Voss sat at one of the room's two tables, seeming fully engrossed in whatever he was reading. The necromancer's bald head gleamed in the magical light and his white robes looked completely out of place in the dark room.

"Voss."

The wizard paused in his reading, his finger stabbing the page to mark his place. Voss focused not on Berend but his new sword. "Zane's been holding out on me. When did he make that?"

"He didn't, he summoned it from Astaroth's hell. I assume a demon did the forging. And speaking of my new equipment, I need some armor. An encounter with a knight's holy sword made it clear my skin isn't adequate on its own."

Voss brightened, which was never a good sign. "I have just the thing, a project I've been working on. You're the perfect one to test it on. How's your pain tolerance?"

"Higher than my magical bullshit tolerance."

Voss swapped his finger for a scrap of paper and closed his book. "Don't worry, Bone Embrace is excellent armor, but getting it properly fit is tricky. There may be some discomfort during the process. Come along and we'll begin."

Berend had a bad feeling but in the end he knew the quality of Voss's work. The armor would no doubt be as useful as it was painful to put on.

If it protected him from holy magic, Berend was willing to make that trade.

CHAPTER 20

D anny left Fishkill at first light. The food at The Tipsy Trout had been decent if a bit greasier than he liked. It was hard to go too far wrong with trout fried in bacon grease. He certainly wouldn't be angry about leaving the stink behind. He'd confirmed with magic a total absence of beastfolk in the town. The few conversations he'd had made it clear they weren't welcome, either as slaves or tourists.

Beastfolk belonged in the mine, that was the local consensus. Obnoxious and ignorant though it might be, their attitude made Danny's task much easier.

Back on the road, he retraced his steps to where he left Briggs the night before. He knew he shouldn't worry about the kid, but he couldn't help himself. At least it was a bit warmer today. Hopefully the worst of winter was behind them. Danny could tolerate the cold, but he didn't enjoy it.

Using the ether to guide him, he reached out for Briggs's presence. He found it soon enough, a bit further away than he expected, but not enough to concern him.

When he entered a clump of trees off to the side of the road, he made sure to make plenty of noise. He doubted Briggs would mistake him for someone else, not with his sharp senses, but why take chances?

A few yards in, the trees opened into a clearing where he found Briggs awake and eating breakfast, an unappealing one of jerky and water. He was kind of slumped over and exhausted looking. Maybe a night on his own hadn't led to the best sleep.

"Did you learn anything?" Briggs asked after swallowing a mouthful of meat.

"Yeah, plenty. Most of it good news for us. All the beastfolk slaves are at the ether crystal mine. The locals have a serious dislike for beastfolk, though the why was never made clear to me. They all acted like it was the most normal thing in the world." Danny shook his head at their irrational way of thinking. "Anyway, how was your night?"

"I had some unwelcome company." Briggs told him about the four men that visited his first camp. "I left their bodies where they lay. Let the crows have them."

He tried to sound tough, but his voice had a slight tremor when he spoke. Had Briggs ever killed someone? Danny didn't know, but from his reaction thought not.

"Are you good to go? I want to try and find the mine today. It's on the far side of the lake in the mountains and that's a fair hike."

Briggs hopped to his feet. "Let's do it."

Danny had too much respect for Briggs to ask any more questions and the two of them set out. He followed the road for a mile or so before turning and heading cross country. The area was open scrubland with lots of paths between clumps of thick bushes. The snow wasn't very deep which helped quite a bit.

Last night in his room, Danny had tried to get an idea of what the weather should be like based on guesstimated latitude and what he'd expect back on Earth. He wasn't sure why he bothered. Nothing about this world lined up with his old one. As best he could figure, Crystal Lake was as far north as Central in the Alliance. Assuming that was right, he felt like it should be colder.

Not that he'd complain about nicer weather. Even after nearly a year this world still struck him as odd. And it no doubt would continue to do so for the rest of his life.

"Why do humans dislike beastfolk so much?" Briggs asked out of nowhere.

"I don't know why *these* humans dislike beastfolk so much. Most of the people I've met had no problem with your people. It seems to be a local issue. I honestly didn't care enough to ask for details. Some people are filled with hate. It's just wired into them. Hell if I can tell you why. Best to avoid them as much as possible."

Danny didn't know if his answer suited Briggs, but he fell into pensive silence and the two jogged on. They rounded the lake around noon before turning toward the mountains.

An hour of walking through thick forest brought them to a rough cart path. Looked like it had been recently used as well. Danny was no master tracker, but even he could tell the ruts in the snow were fresh.

"I hope it's not more guards," Briggs said.

"Doubtful. More likely it's some merchants coming to pick up a load of crystals. Either way we're getting close. I can feel the ether sparking up ahead. That's got to be the ether pool. It's little more than a mile ahead."

Briggs clenched his fists but said nothing as they continued on. Danny kept the pace slow and all his senses alert. There was no way such a valuable location wasn't defended. Not that he was overly concerned with normal guards. He could take out any number of them without breaking a sweat. It was collateral damage from an errant spell that worried him most. Either that or the guards taking a hostage.

As they approached the mine, the forest thinned and finally ended at the base of two sheer cliffs. Danny stopped well back, out of sight. He peered around a chunky pine tree at a tall wooden wall with a wide gate built between the cliffs which controlled access to the area beyond. Four huge figures prowled along the battlements, heavy crossbows clutched in their hands. There was no way those were humans. They had to be nearly eight feet tall.

Briggs eased up beside him. "What are those?"

Danny shook his head. "They're not big enough for ogres, but they're too big for men. Some kind of half-breeds maybe. Doesn't really matter what they are. We have to deal with them regardless. At least I can't sense any corruption, that means no demons."

"Thank heaven for small favors," Briggs said. "What's the plan?"

"Can you turn invisible and leap over the wall?"

Briggs cocked his head, frowned, then said, "Grimshadow says it's too high, but if you can get inside, I can teleport in to join you. I won't be able to use that ability for a while afterwards."

The last thing Danny wanted was to weaken the kid before the fighting started. "Okay, plan B. I'll go up there, take out the guards, and open a passage for you. We need to deal with them anyway, might as well do it now as later."

"I hate relying on you for everything."

"You're not. I'd need to get in there with or without you. Once the slaves are free, protecting them will be your job. I'll be busy trying to find the ether pool. I have no idea what will happen after I destroy it, but I'm worried about the release of the pent-up energy. You'll need to take everyone as far away as you can."

"What about you?"

"I'm tougher than I look. Just go. I'll catch up with you as soon as I can. Hang on."

Danny activated his stealth field and broke cover. A quick sprint brought him to the base of the wall. He looked up, trying to gauge the height. Maybe forty feet? It wasn't as high as the wall around Villipan and he'd cleared that one easily enough.

Gathering ether in his legs, Danny sprang straight up. He was nearly at the top when his momentum started to run out. Hardening his fingers, Danny dug them into the wood and swung himself up and over the top onto the battlements. The nearest guards were completely unaware of his presence.

Best to get this over with quickly. Danny drew his sword and lunged right, striking with every bit of enhanced speed and strength he could manage.

He cut through the guard's thick neck and sent his head tumbling to the ground. Hot blood spurted and his body crumpled.

He had to take the others out quickly. The death of their comrade hadn't gone unnoticed and the last thing he wanted was for someone to raise the alarm.

Luckily for Danny, if there was one thing he was good at, it was moving quickly. He cut the next guard down a second later and was soon sprinting back toward the other side of the wall.

One guard got a shot off, missing him by several feet, before getting cut in half.

The final guard drew a breath to shout.

Danny gathered ether and hurled a fist of pure force that struck the guard in the head, crushing his skull to pulp.

And that was it. Danny leapt down, moved to the edge of the wall, and took the ethersword out of storage. It took only a moment to slice an opening big enough for Briggs to enter.

Danny stepped out and waved him over. Briggs broke cover, sprinted over, and they ducked back through the opening.

"That was... something. Even after your spell ended, I could barely follow your movements. How easy were you taking it on me during our sparring match?"

"Let's discuss it later. We need to move quickly, before anyone notices the guards are gone. We'll clear the buildings one at a time. We can't take prisoners. You understand what that means, right?"

"I swore I'd do whatever it takes to find and free my mother and the others and I meant it. A bunch of dead slave-keepers isn't going to hurt my feelings any."

"Good."

Danny led the way into the compound. There were half a dozen outbuildings including one that looked like someone's house. It was so out of place compared to all the other rough shacks, he wasn't sure what to make of it.

He'd deal with it when he had to. First up was a long, low building running along a steep stone wall. It was built out of crumbled stone, leftover boards, and tree limbs. Danny figured a good kick would be enough to send it tumbling to the ground.

He reached the door and kicked it open. The white glow of the ethersword revealed a double row of rough cots. Looked like a barracks for the slaves. Pity no one was home. Not that he expected to find anyone kicking back and relaxing in the middle of the afternoon.

"This is awful." Briggs had Grimshadow in hand and his knuckles were white on the grip.

"At least they're not sleeping in the mine. Bad as this is, the cold stone would be harder on them."

Danny left the barracks and went to the next building, a smaller, slightly better built place on the same line as the slave quarters. This one lacked gaps in the walls at least, though that was about all he could say in its favor.

A swift kick sent the door crashing open. Inside, half-awake guards groaned and tried to get out of bed.

Danny had no intention of giving them the chance. He ran in, ethersword leading. To call the slaughter that followed a fight would be overly generous, but the job was done and no alarm was raised. Briggs just stood in the doorway trembling. Killing people with the ethersword wasn't a pretty process. The unstoppable blade tended to leave pieces behind wherever it passed.

"Snap out of it." Danny gave him a shake. "This is war, albeit on a small scale. The enemy needs to die and our job is to kill them. If you can't do it, I recommend letting Grimshadow take over your body, at least until the fighting is finished. I'll make sure he gives it back."

He hadn't meant to be quite so hard on the kid, but this was no time to be spacing out. If Briggs couldn't fight, he was a liability. Danny couldn't do what he needed to and protect him at the same time.

Grimshadow's leather grip creaked as Briggs squeezed it with all his might. "I can do it, I promise. That was just more intense than I expected. No wonder the Reaper likes you. I've never seen anyone kill like you did."

Danny wasn't sure that was a compliment, but he didn't have time to talk about it now. He left the dead guards behind and set out for the next building. This was the best built of the bunch outside of the house further up. It had a heavy timber frame and a slate roof. The door looked thick enough to stop a couple of blows from a battering ram. The ethereal currents flowed oddly around the building but when Danny activated a detection spell he saw no traps.

He shrugged, strengthened his personal shield and strode over. Three quick strokes reduced the door to kindling. Inside, human and beastfolk slaves were chained to long tables where they stood quietly staring at Danny. Four men in fine robes were gaping like freshly caught fish, their mouths working but no noise coming out.

"Who the hell are you?" roared a huge man, assuming he was actually human. He carried an ax that had to weigh thirty pounds and wore no shirt despite the cold. Like all the others Danny had seen, this one had patches of scaly green skin mingled with the smooth, pale flesh you'd expect on a human.

Danny didn't bother to answer. A blast of lightning strengthened via the mithril hilt slammed into the big guy and sent him tumbling into the back wall.

The fancy men threw their hands up. "Please don't hurt us. Take all the crystals you want."

Danny had a strong suspicion that these fellows were

merchants with Crystal Veil Trading. He was debating what to do with them when Briggs shouted, "Mom!" and rushed past him.

Briggs ran over to one of the chained-up beastfolk women and hugged her.

Content to let the pair have a moment, he walked over to the possible merchants. "The mine is out of business, gentlemen. You can leave and never come back or you can die where you stand. What will it be?"

One of the men shoved to the fore. "Do you have any idea who we are?"

"My working theory is someone associated with Crystal Veil Trading. You certainly don't look like slavedrivers or guards. That's the only reason I'm considering letting you go. Had you been directly responsible for the poor conditions these people are kept in, I'd have happily killed you all."

"So you're not a complete fool. My name is Merowin Sibil and I'm the third-ranking member of the company in charge of mine negotiations. We make tens of thousands of gold coins selling ether crystals all over the continent. You can't possibly imagine we'll just stop because you tell us to. Even if you free the slaves and kill Vulmar and his thugs, new slaves will be brought in and new soldiers will mind them. You accomplish nothing beyond making an enemy of the richest merchant company in the region. I swear you'll be dead by the end of the week. We have a small army working for us. You have no—"

Merowin fell silent when Danny put the tip of the ether-sword an inch from the hollow of his throat. "Are you quite finished?"

The merchant started to nod then thought better of it.

"Now you need to listen to me. Everything you said may

be true. I can't predict the future, though I can promise you that, should a single Crystal Veil soldier come after me, I'll return and burn every building you own to the ground with the merchants still inside. I'm not sure what sort of people you're used to bullying with your pitiful threats, but none of them is as strong as me. Here's my advice. Find a way to make a living that doesn't require you to chain your employees to a table. Now get lost."

He lowered the ethersword and the merchants hastened to flee. Would he come to regret letting them go? Maybe, but those men weren't warriors and killing merchants, even scumbag ones, didn't appeal to Danny. Should they declare war on him, he'd return the favor, but for now he was content to forget about them.

"Ronin." He turned to find Briggs sitting beside his mother. She, along with all the other slaves, were staring at him. "This is my mom. She says the rest of our pack is in the mine."

"I figured. Pleasure to meet you, ma'am. Let's get those chains off everyone." Danny conjured an ethereal key and used it to pop the locks one by one until all the slaves were free. "There we go. Does anyone need healing?"

They all kept staring silently as if in a daze. Perhaps they were unable to accept their freedom. He didn't know but didn't waste the time it would take to convince them.

He slipped past the slaves into the back room. As he thought, the shelves were lined with leather pouches no doubt filled to the brim with ether crystals. Never one to waste resources, Danny collected them all and put them into his storage. They'd make a convenient source of funding on his journey. That done, he returned to the main room.

"Okay, I'm heading to the mine. You guys stay here. I'll

send the slaves this way as I free them. Once I'm done, it'll be up to you to protect everyone." Danny addressed the last line to Briggs, who nodded. "Remember, once the last slave is out, move as far from the mine as you can as fast as you can. I'll catch up as soon as I'm able."

"I remember," Briggs said. "And thank you again for getting me this far."

"You did plenty on your own." Danny clapped him on the arm, turned, and marched out of the warmth and toward the mine.

He'd clear the house and remaining building first, but from a distance it didn't feel like anyone was inside. No doubt he would be less lucky at the mine itself. But that was fine. He'd deal with whatever he had to. So far he hadn't run into anything too worrisome.

Danny wouldn't complain if it stayed that way.

CHAPTER 21

Briggs watched Ronin until he was out of sight, then returned to his mother. She was awfully thin, had a few bumps and bruises, and was in serious need of a bath, but otherwise appeared unharmed after her time as a slave, thank goodness. If anything had happened to her...

He let the thought trail off. Best not to think about that. She was okay and nothing else mattered.

The other slaves were still staring around as if not quite believing what had happened. Briggs knew how they felt. Ronin had that effect wherever he went.

"Your human friend is an interesting fellow," his mother said. "How did you ever end up in his company?"

"He saved me from some humans who thought I was carrying the plague. He's friends with Val and it sounds like he offered to keep an eye out for us on his travels. I wouldn't have made it this far without his help."

"Val's okay?" His mother brightened, flashing a smile he hadn't seen in far too long.

Briggs nodded. "Maybe I should tell you everything."

She nodded and he shared all that had happened since he met Ronin. He glossed over just how nasty Grimshadow was. After all she'd been through, the last thing he wanted to do was upset her further.

When he finished Briggs added, "Ronin's going to try and destroy the source of the ether crystals. If he can, the humans won't need beastfolk slaves to dig them up."

Her smile twisted into something less pleasant. "They'll always be after us for something. It's the way of the world. The packs will need to find better places to hide."

"How come you didn't end up in the mine?" Briggs asked.

"They tested each of us to see how agile our hands were. The best were given the task of separating the crystals from the chunks of stone the miners dug up. It was hard, but far better than digging. At least we were warm. The guards didn't want our hands getting numb and risk breaking a crystal. If you did that, it earned you a beating. It seemed like at least once a week one of the miners would end up carried out of the mine. It's a small wonder they need so many slaves."

Speaking of, the rest of the slaves were muttering amongst themselves. There was no one from Briggs's pack among the others. While he was glad to free them, they weren't family and so weren't to be trusted. He kept a wary eye on them, his hand never far from Grimshadow's hilt.

You were far too slow during the fight. I didn't get anything to eat.

Briggs ignored the always-hungry demon. Sometimes he thought he could murder the world and it wouldn't be enough for him.

"What are we going to do now?" one of the humans asked.

Briggs turned to look at him and the man flinched as if expecting to be slapped. "We're going to wait for the rest of the slaves to be freed then we're going to leave this place. You're welcome to travel with us until we reach human territory."

"This is human territory," said one of the beastfolk, an older female from an unknown pack. "Let them take their chances with their own kind. We owe them nothing."

"That's right," another beastwoman said. "Humans are the ones who kidnapped us in the first place."

"And a human helped free you," Briggs said. "You'd still be in those chains if not for Ronin. I used to hate all humans for what the soldiers did to us, but that was wrong. Hate the ones who captured you and brought you here. Hate the ones who made you work. But don't hate them because of what they are, hate them for what they did."

His mother ruffled his hair. "When did you become wise?"

"I didn't, not really. I just had a chance to get to know Ronin. He's nothing like other humans I've encountered. He treated me like a member of his pack. I still don't know why. As far as I can tell I've done nothing to help him with his mission. He's an odd human."

Briggs cocked his head. He sensed someone approaching through his link with Grimshadow. "Stay away from the door. Someone's coming."

He could feel the others' anxiety but didn't let it distract him. He drew Grimshadow and peeked out the ruined doorway. Six ragged beastfolk, their meager clothing torn and their bodies filthy, were running his way.

Briggs relaxed and put Grimshadow away before waving them over. They waved back and altered their course. When they reached him, the oldest, a beastman Val's age, asked, "Are you Briggs? The human who freed us said to join you."

Briggs nodded. "That's me. As soon as Ronin frees everyone, I'll guide you to safety."

"You're barely more than a pup," one of the others said.

"You're not wrong. Should you prefer to take your chances on your own, feel free to help yourselves to the dead guards' weapons. There's a gap in the wall you can use to escape."

The first beastman frowned. "You wouldn't try and stop us?"

Briggs shrugged. "You're not members of my pack. What do I care if you get yourselves killed? That's our way, is it not? Each pack tends to its own territory. We don't interfere with each other. The humans rely on us staying weak and separate. One pack is no problem for them. All of us together would make them think twice."

"The packs have never worked together," the older beastman said.

"Maybe it's time we gave it a try." Briggs held out his hand.

The beastman hesitated then gripped his hand in the traditional way. "Maybe it is. We will stick with you. But first, where are those weapons you mentioned? We will not become slaves again."

Briggs directed them to the barracks and they hurried off. He turned to find his mother smiling with pride. It was a good feeling, though he feared he was overstepping himself. Maybe Val would call him a fool when they met up. But that was okay with Briggs, because it meant they did meet up.

He looked toward the mine and found three more slaves headed his way. It came as no surprise that Ronin was working quickly. From what he'd seen, there was nothing that could even slow the human, much less defeat him.

Briggs dearly hoped they didn't run into anything on the road. He would do his best to keep everyone safe, but he was no Ronin.

CHAPTER 22

Danny sent the last two slaves running, or limping if you wanted to be accurate about it, back toward the mine exit. The guards ended up being more of the mixed-race humans he fought on his way here. Against chained-up slaves they were quite impressive. Against Danny, they were walking corpses.

The ether was especially chaotic in the mine. He figured the crystals and ether pool were responsible for that. Fortunately, he was still able to use his magic without issue. And that magic assured him no living things remained down here. He had to be confident Briggs would escort everyone to safety. His job now was to find the ether pool and make sure no one could ever use it again.

The problem was, he wasn't exactly sure how. The rough stone walls of the mine looked perfectly normal. He'd seen no hint of a door or other artificial structure. He assumed the elf-bloods would've hidden it. The questioned was, where?

The ether pool's job was to draw in and store magical

energy. Assuming he was right, it had to act like a vacuum. Hopefully he could follow the current of ether right to it.

He focused his magical vision on the ether. It looked like swirls and random bursts of blue light here. If it had a current, he couldn't see it. At least not yet. Moving slowly down the tunnel, he kept his focus on the lights. If someone attacked him now, he'd be in trouble. Which was why he'd made sure to confirm the absence of others.

It was just him and the ether.

He turned down a narrow, left-branching tunnel and paused. A thin ripple ran straight down the passage. That was the first sign of anything even vaguely orderly he'd seen. Maybe it was nothing and maybe it was something, but either way he couldn't ignore it.

Keeping a close eye on his guide, he continued down the tunnel. It gradually started sloping down. The walls were still rough, but the marks didn't look like they'd been made by picks. They almost looked like claw marks.

Danny shuddered. He had no desire to encounter whatever dug this passage out. Hopefully it had been dead for at least a thousand years.

A hundred yards further on, a second ripple joined the first. He was definitely on the right path.

The further Danny ventured, the more ripples appeared, converging into a steady stream that flowed through the air like an ethereal river. Eventually it grew to the point that the light was bright enough to see even without using detection magic. It cast a sapphire-blue light on the claw-marked walls.

He had to be getting close.

Fifty yards further on, the tunnel stopped. A smooth stone wall blocked him from taking another step.

Danny swallowed a curse. This couldn't be the end of the

path. Nothing about the wall looked natural. Even the stone was the wrong color; it was a lighter gray than the rest.

He snarled and punched the wall with the ethersword's hilt. Cracks ran through the stone and a moment later a four-inch-thick fake wall crumbled, leaving him staring at polished steel. Steel that looked exactly like the towers in Elfhome.

A couple more blows removed the last of the stone cover, but he saw no way past the wall. He'd assumed there'd be a door-activation rune somewhere, but he couldn't find anything in either his normal or magical vision. Well, if subtlety couldn't do the trick, he'd try something more direct. Danny drew back and slammed the tip of the ether-sword into the wall.

It resisted for a moment, then, slowly, a millimeter at a time, the blade cut it. He didn't know how long it took, but eventually the resistance vanished. He pulled back and found a perfectly round blade-sized hole. An eerie blue glow the same color as the ripple he'd been following emerged from the opening. Danny pressed his eye to the hole for a closer look.

What he found was less remarkable than he'd expected. The source of the light was a circle of runes surrounding a pit maybe fifteen paces in diameter. A matching glow came from the bottom of the pit. The chamber itself was solid steel lacking any sort of decoration. The elf-bloods seemed to be minimalists when it came to their spaces. You'd think being descended from Heaven they'd have statues of the archangels or something.

Well, whatever. An empty chamber was a lot safer than one guarded by demons or whatever the elf-blood equivalent was.

Cutting through the wall wasn't a speedy process. Whatever the elf-bloods had done to their steel made it resist the ethersword's disintegration effect nearly as well as Hell-forged black iron.

Inch by inch, Danny cut a doorway in the wall. The process took most of half an hour but when it was complete the section of wall fell in with an awful clank. There was no reaction and when silence settled over the chamber once more it seemed even quieter.

Danny stepped through the newly carved opening, the clanging of his boots sounding like gongs against the polished steel floor. The air inside the chamber was stale with a sort of ionized feel he attributed to the heavy concentration of ether. The blue glow emanating from the pit gave the room an unnatural vibe that made the hair on Danny's arms stand on end.

He approached the edge of the pit but stopped short of the rune circle. Peering down into its depths he could make out nothing beyond the glow. If there was a bottom it was either out of sight or hidden by the light. He further assumed the line connecting the pool to the cathedral in Villipan was down there somewhere. If it was as deep as the line under Elfhome, that gave him a rough idea how deep the pit ran.

Far enough that he didn't want to fall in.

The question now was, how best to destroy it? Slashing through the runes would probably do the job, but he wanted to be sure no one could repair the damage. Then again, anyone capable of doing so was long dead. Since he saw no other options, he raised the ethersword and slammed the blade down on the rune circle.

It bounced off without leaving a mark.

The blue light filling the room turned red and a rumble

ran through the floor. Three sections of wall dropped into the ground and huge metal constructs rolled out on steel wheels. The bodies looked vaguely wormlike, but the claws out front screamed lobster.

So much for avoiding whatever dug the tunnel.

A voice from nowhere started issuing warnings in Elvish. At least Danny assumed they were warnings. He didn't have the power to waste on a translation spell.

All three diggers oriented on him and advanced at a steady rumble.

Danny had no interest in getting surrounded.

He charged the right-hand digger, leapt a swipe from one of its claws, and slashed its flank. The ethersword left a half-inch-deep groove that didn't trouble the construct at all.

At least it wasn't fast. If the thing had been as quick as it was tough, Danny would've been in trouble. Or, worse trouble anyway.

Danny dodged another swipe from the digger's claw. Fighting this thing was like going to war with a bulldozer and excavator that had been welded together. It had to have a weak point. Maybe if he hacked off the arms. There was a joint in the middle that let the claw swing. Looked like a promising target.

A quick jump back kept Danny from getting flattened as the digger's claw smashed into the floor.

He darted around to the side, aiming for the arm joint.

The blade sank in a few inches before the digger swung its arm, sending him flying across the chamber. One of its friends tried to run Danny over the moment he landed. A backflip carried him clear but left him off balance.

A backhand swipe of the second digger's arm slammed into Danny and sent him flying once more. He crashed into the wall with a grunt of pain as the air was knocked out of him.

Heaven's mercy, he would've preferred to fight a small army of demons to these things.

Forcing himself to his feet, Danny grimaced and ignored the pain. He could heal himself if he survived.

All three diggers were closing in on him and he had the wall at his back. Not exactly an ideal position. He needed to end this fast before the diggers overwhelmed him through sheer relentlessness.

It was time to stop screwing around.

Danny pushed his physical enhancements to the next level and darted forward. The diggers appeared to be moving even slower now.

He lashed out with the ethersword.

Once.

Twice.

Three times.

The first arm clanged to the floor.

That was the trick. Hit the same spot over and over until you got through.

He repeated the process on the second arm. The blows came so fast they sounded like machine-gun fire.

In seconds the digger was disarmed, literally.

Danny charged the second construct, hacking its arms off in a blur of blows.

His body started to ache as the enhancements took their toll. Just one left, then he could back off again.

Danny took a deep breath and leaped at the third digger. A flurry of lightning-fast strikes chipped away at the arm joints until the final claw crashed to the floor.

Danny staggered back out of the diggers' way lest he get

run over instead. His chest heaved as he gulped in deep breaths. He let his physical enhancements fade to a minimal level and studied his opponents.

What would they do now?

He didn't have to wait long to find out. The diggers turned their worm-like bodies toward Danny, their wheels screeching on the floor. The warning voice continued to blare in Elvish. It was more annoying than the constructs, but he couldn't figure out how to stop it. It wasn't like there were speakers he could smash.

Danny tensed, ethersword at the ready, as the diggers rolled closer. Without arms, their tactics had changed. They seemed intent on herding him toward the wall and crushing him. Danny darted out of the way as the first one rumbled past, and slashed its side, cutting another shallow groove.

The second followed close behind its partner, trying to cut off his escape.

Danny leaped, landed on the digger's back, and drove the ethersword into it with all his might. It slowly sank in to the hilt with no noticeable effect on the construct.

The digger thrashed, trying to shake him off to no avail.

This thing had to have a core, something that controlled and powered it. Stabbing at random wasn't doing him any good. He needed to find the right spot.

Danny's perch was secure for the moment, so he risked a glance at the ether pit. Still glowing red, but no other changes. That was a relief. He had enough to deal with as it was.

Returning his full attention to the diggers, he focused on their bodies, trying see how the ether flowed around and through them. It wasn't easy to concentrate while basically riding a giant mechanical bull, but he did his best.

It looked like the diggers weren't connected to the ether itself. That was good since it meant they had to have a magical power source somewhere within. If Danny could destroy that, hopefully it would mean they'd stop moving.

Locating it within the constructs, especially given how much ether was in the chamber, was no mean feat.

An especially sharp jerk tried to dislocate his shoulder and succeeded in widening the gash he'd cut in the digger. Another foot and he'd be in danger of losing his handhold.

Silently cursing elf-bloods in general and whoever made these things in particular, Danny began a methodical scan of their bodies. Minutes passed as his gaze slowly shifted down the length of the tubular body. At the halfway point he saw something. A slightly denser spot of ether.

That had to be it. Unfortunately, it was at the thickest point of the digger. No way could he reach it with the ethersword.

Come on, think!

There had to be a way to destroy it.

A moment later he snapped his fingers. He could overload the core and make it explode or shatter or whatever it did when it collected too much power.

As soon as he made up his mind, Danny began channeling ether directly into the core. The construct thrashed even more violently, threatening to throw him off. It slammed into the wall head on as it went berserk. The reaction only encouraged Danny to continue forcing more power into it.

The digger started to vibrate and its skin or whatever it was covered in grew hot. Maybe doing this while standing on its back hadn't been the best idea.

With a shuddering groan, the digger lurched to a halt. The surface was too hot to touch now. Danny wrenched the ethersword free and leapt clear a moment before the construct detonated. A blinding flash of ether filled the air and when it vanished the digger had been reduced to slag.

At least there hadn't been any shrapnel.

Now for the other two.

As if summoned by the thought the remaining diggers charged him from opposite directions.

Danny gathered himself and leapt onto the nearest construct's back. He barely got the ethersword buried in its metal flesh before the two constructs hammered into each other. It took all he had not to lose his place.

Setting himself, he found the digger's core and flooded it with ether. Now that he knew the process it went faster. Soon the construct began to shudder and convulse. Its metallic skin grew scorching to the touch.

Danny yanked the ethersword free and vaulted off its back just ahead of the explosion of blinding blue light. When it faded the digger had been reduce to so much melted scrap metal.

The final digger barreled toward him, its armless body screeching across the steel floor. Weakened as he was, Danny barely rolled out of the way in time to avoid getting crushed.

He channeled ether into its core, pouring it in as fast as he could. His efforts had the unintended side effect of speeding its movement. The digger slammed into the wall, backed up way faster than it should've, and slammed into another wall. It reminded Danny of his younger brother when he first got his license.

It was shaking and shuddering as it finally lined up with him. The wheels barely started to turn when the core exploded and slagged the digger.

When half a minute passed and nothing else tried to kill

him, Danny gave in to the overwhelming urge to sit down. The screeching Elvish warning finally ended as well. The message must've been connected to the diggers. It was a mystery that didn't overly interest him.

For now he needed to rest, then he'd find a way to destroy the rune circle. Hopefully it wouldn't be as difficult to deal with as the diggers.

CHAPTER 23

A lot of people thought hating was a bad thing, but not Nash Veil. He thoroughly enjoyed hating things. It was one of the reasons he worshipped Astaroth. Demon lords encouraged hate and Nash needed no encouragement. The only thing he enjoyed more than hating things was destroying them.

That was why he found visiting the ether crystal mine so frustrating. He utterly despised Vulmar and his filthy operation, yet he wasn't free to destroy the place and kill everyone. Hating useful things was a pain.

He sighed and turned up the path to the mine. Best to fetch the crystals Zane needed and leave as quickly as possible. He was only human after all. His self-control wasn't limitless. One too many comments from Vulmar and he was likely to do something that would inconvenience the group.

So he strode up the dirt path he regularly swore he'd never walk again. The faint chill didn't bother him. The worst of the winter cold was over and his light cloak kept him plenty warm.

A hundred yards further on Nash froze and cocked his head. Footsteps were headed his way. Three, no four sets, walking slowly. Soft voices as well. There hadn't been a slave auction in months, so it wasn't a dealer returning from a delivery. The only other group it might be was the merchants they allowed to sell whatever crystals were unsuitable for the group's use.

Nash didn't hate the merchants. They were insects barely worth his notice. Still, best make sure they hadn't claimed any of the large crystals. Coming up short would do nothing to improve his mood.

Five minutes later the merchants appeared from around a short curve. The first robed figure flinched when he saw Nash. Not an uncommon reaction given his empty eye sockets. To his credit the merchant recovered quickly.

"Lord Veil, you startled me. If you're going to the mine, I must warn you there's a crazy man there with a glowing sword killing the guards. We're on our way back to Crystal Veil's headquarters to organize our mercenaries to reclaim the mine."

Nash grimaced, both because of the news and at hearing his name used as if it belonged to the merchant company. Why he had ever agreed to act as the company's figurehead was beyond him. No, that wasn't true. Zane had told him to do it and so he did, just like he did whatever Zane said. It was an annoying habit of his, but when you followed a demon lord, you were obliged to obey their priests, at least to a certain extent.

"I'll deal with the interloper," Nash said. "Wait at least a day before you disrupt our schedule. Should I fall, I leave it up to you to decide how best to proceed."

The merchant looked like he wanted to argue but it

passed and he bowed. "As you say, Lord Veil. We'll be on our way."

The little knot of uselessness hurried past Nash and he immediately forgot them. As he resumed his walk he debated who the mystery swordsman might be. Surely even he would remember an enemy who wielded a glowing sword.

Nash shrugged and adjusted his own slightly curved blade. He'd find out who it was soon enough. Guessing would accomplish nothing.

○

Briggs stood in the doorway of the sorting hut and kept his gaze trained on the mine entrance. It had been a little while since any beastfolk emerged and all the miners were beastfolk, mostly males but a few stronger females. Over a hundred badly treated individuals from a dozen packs were crowded into the hut. It wasn't a comfortable situation, which was part of the reason he was in the doorway.

A few of the more recent arrivals had spoken with him and to a person they described Ronin like he was a vision of the Reaper. None of the guards even slowed him down. Hunters who had fought Alpha Wolves trembled when they described it.

Briggs wanted to argue with them, explain the sort of person Ronin was, but in the end he didn't bother. Having seen his human friend fight, he understood their fear and no words would change their first impression.

He was about to suggest they move out when two more slaves emerged from the entrance. One of them was limping and leaning on the other as they came along at the best speed they could manage.

When they reached the hut the uninjured beastman said, "Are you Briggs?"

"That's right."

"The human who freed us said to tell you we're the last."

Briggs blew out a breath of relief. "Are you strong enough to keep moving? We need to put as much distance between ourselves and this place as we can. I'm surprised Ronin didn't offer to heal you."

The lame beastman couldn't look him in the eye. "He did. I feared his magic and said I was unharmed. Foolish, but in the moment, I could do nothing else."

"We won't slow you down, I promise," the second beastman said.

Briggs understood the injured beastman's trepidation, baseless as it was, and said nothing about it. He turned to address the ragged group huddled behind him. "It's time to go. We'll collect what weapons we can find on our way out."

No one complained about leaving this place behind and they set out with him in the lead. Briggs doubted they'd run into anything too dangerous as long as they stayed away from the human towns. Animals would avoid a group this big. Eventually he'd have to leave the group to hunt, but that would keep until they'd put some distance between themselves and the mine. Hopefully Ronin would catch up quickly.

Briggs led the way out. They swung by the barracks and picked up spears for all those able to wield them. That brought their numbers up to twenty armed warriors. Granted, they were battered and weakened warriors, but they were also determined not to return to slavery. Their determination would make them stronger should it come to a fight.

They also collected bags of preserved meat and anything else that looked edible. The noncombatants were tasked with carrying the supplies.

Ready as they'd ever be, Briggs led them in the direction of the gate. Since he had no idea how the opening mechanism worked, he angled the group toward the opening Ronin had cut in the wall. They could leave single file.

He glanced back over his shoulder and found the compound quiet.

Don't worry about Ronin. That human is stronger than all of you combined and not by a small amount.

Grimshadow was right, he knew that, but couldn't help worrying about his friend. Ronin had done so much for him. The idea of leaving him to face whatever was waiting under the mine on his own seemed wrong.

Forget Ronin, we've got issues of our own.

Briggs spun around and frowned as an eyeless human stepped through the wall gap in front of them. He carried a sword but wore no armor. A light cloak fluttered in the breeze as he turned his head to look from person to person.

For a person with no eyes, he certainly acted like he could see.

He's using magic to see. Don't underestimate this one.

"Where do you slaves think you're going?" the eyeless man asked.

Before Briggs could answer, one of the more aggrieved beastmen said, "We're not slaves anymore. Stand aside or die like Vulmar and his guards."

"Vulmar's dead? How lovely, though I would've preferred to kill him myself. If there's one thing I've learned it's that life is full of disappointment. Another example is you lot thinking you're free. You're not. You have two choices. One, return to your barracks and wait for new guards to arrive. Two, attempt to leave, be killed by me, and rise again as a zombie. Either way, you will be digging ether crystals for us in short order."

"Like hell we will!" Four beastmen charged the swordsman.

They managed three strides before his blade leapt out of its sheath and flew toward them. It flashed once and the lead beastman collapsed, his head neatly severed from his neck.

A subtle gesture from the swordsman's right hand sent his sword racing around to slash the others to pieces. The whole process took seconds.

A final gesture returned the blade to its sheath. "Anyone else?"

Briggs steeled himself. This was going to be the hardest fight of his life, he had no doubt about it. But there was no other choice if they wanted to get out of here.

He drew Grimshadow and stepped forward. "We have no fight with you. We only wish to be free."

The human nodded. "I have no doubt that's true. Most slaves wish to be free. As an owner and employer of slaves, I couldn't possibly care less what you want. It's a bit like my sword claiming it doesn't want to kill people. My property isn't allowed an opinion about how I use it."

Briggs had only an instant of warning before the sword came flying out at him. His enhanced speed allowed him to dodge at the last moment. The sword whipped past his neck, curving through the air like a snake before doubling back for another strike.

He parried with Grimshadow, sparks flying as the blades

clashed. The sword was quick, but didn't have any real weight behind it.

And thank goodness for that small favor.

The eyeless human's fingers twitched, guiding the sword's movements as it darted and slashed at Briggs from impossible angles.

Briggs grimaced at another close call. He couldn't win like this. He needed to close the distance.

Maybe if he went invisible.

Don't bother. His magical eyes would still be able to see you.

Briggs blocked the incoming sword and sent it flying. "I'm open to suggestions."

Just charge him. I'll warn you if the sword is coming from your blind spot.

Putting his life in Grimshadow's hands was every bit as risky as fighting the swordsman on his own. But it wasn't like he had another option.

Briggs kicked the ground hard and charged.

He ran straight at the human, hoping to close the distance as quickly as possible. Out of the corner of his eye Briggs saw the sword coming in from his right.

He twisted and dodged at the last second.

The blade sliced his tunic but missed the skin beneath.

Only a few more strides.

Briggs lunged and slashed at the swordsman's neck. Somehow the sword had returned to the man's hand in time to let him block. A hard shove sent Briggs flying back.

"I'm impressed. I can't remember the last time anyone, much less a beastman, forced me to wield my sword with my own hand. Other than Berend of course, but he hardly counts since neither of us was trying to kill the other with any real enthusiasm."

Briggs remained silent, trying to catch his breath.

"You're not worn out already, are you?" the human asked. "I was hoping you might entertain me a bit more."

"I'm nowhere near done."

Briggs darted in, slashing high before spinning to thrust at his opponent's chest.

The blow was turned aside with contemptuous ease. The swordsman's blade flashed out, nearly taking Briggs's arm off at the elbow. Only a desperate twist saved him.

Briggs leapt back, skidded to a halt, and rushed forward again. Another flurry of attacks got him nowhere. At this rate he'd be exhausted before he put so much as a scratch on the man.

He only had one option left.

Short-range teleportation is risky.

Briggs didn't need the warning. He'd only used Grimshadow's strongest ability once and it had left him near vomiting for ten minutes. Something about the magic messed with his senses. But he saw no other option if he wanted to win.

"You're really hanging in there," the swordsman said. "This is the most fun I've had in years."

Briggs bared his teeth in a snarl. No matter what it took he swore he'd shove the human's arrogance down his throat.

He charged in again.

As soon as the human shifted his sword to block, Briggs called on Grimshadow's magic.

The world blurred and then he appeared directly behind the swordsman.

The human turned, quick as a flash, and slashed.

Too slow.

Briggs teleported a second time and rammed

Grimshadow through the man's side and into his heart. The look of shocked disbelief that flitted across his face would warm Briggs's heart for the rest of his days.

The human collapsed and Briggs hit his knees soon after. If he had to fight again any time soon, they were all in a lot of trouble.

"Briggs!" His mother hurried over and knelt beside him. "Are you hurt?"

"Just tired, Mom. Don't worry. Help me up."

"You should rest some more," she said.

"I wish I could, but we need to put some distance between us and the mine. I'm not sure what Ronin is going to do, but he feared the reaction would be violent. And if he was worried, we should be terrified. I'd like to manage at least a few miles before dark."

She gave him one last worried look then nodded. She took his hand and pulled him to his feet. Briggs's legs wobbled but he didn't fall again. That had to be a good sign.

A moment later strength rushed through him. After a moment of confusion Grimshadow's voice appeared in his mind.

I've shared some of the life force I took from the human. It will last you a few hours. Long enough to get somewhere safe.

Briggs wasn't about to complain. He led the procession of former slaves through the gap in the wall. Hopefully they could move far enough away before Ronin did whatever he had to.

CHAPTER 24

A three-hour rest did wonders to restore Danny's strength. He hopped to his feet and marched around one of the ruined diggers to the rune circle. Despite everything he'd done, nothing appeared to have changed. The ether had gone back to glowing blue and the Elvish recording hadn't resumed.

He stopped at the edge of the rune circle and looked around. As far as he could tell there was nowhere else for anything to come from. The prospect of another fight to the death didn't appeal to him.

Danny shrugged and lit the ethersword. One way to find out for sure.

He slammed the blade into the rune circle and once again it bounced off. The ether turned red and the Elvish voice started repeating its spiel.

When a minute passed and nothing else happened Danny activated a translation spell. "Warning! Damaging the rune circle risks rendering this ethereal line inoperative and triggering a catastrophic release of stored ether. Discontinue all efforts to damage the circle."

The same message repeated over and over again confirming that his actions would get the result he wanted. Nice of the elf-bloods to offer that reassurance.

Now, how to actually damage the runes? If chopping the runes didn't work, maybe slowly cutting through would. He laid the edge of the ethersword on the circle, pressed firmly, and waited.

Time ticked away, but Danny kept his patience despite the obnoxious voice.

Two minutes in, he felt it. The blade shifted a fraction deeper. Ethereal lightning leapt out of the pool, sparking around the room as the light faded in and out like a shorted-out Christmas tree.

The voice changed, becoming less strident and more panicked. "Warning! Warning! Containment rune breach. Ethereal evacuation imminent."

Right, time to go.

Danny deactivated the ethersword, slipped it into storage, and ran for the hole he'd made in the wall. As soon as he hit the dark tunnel, he swapped the translation spell for a dark vision spell.

He ran as fast as he could while avoiding rough spots and bodies. All around him the ether grew ever more chaotic. The heat rose as well and soon Danny was sweating.

He ignored everything except putting as much distance between himself and the ether pool as possible.

When he finally spotted the exit, the tunnel was shaking and rocks were falling out of the ceiling. A small boulder glanced off his shoulder, drawing a wince but doing no real damage through his personal shield.

And then he was outside and sprinting through the mine

camp. He sensed no life which meant Briggs had gotten all the beastfolk out. They should be miles from here by now. He glanced at the shadows. With the mountains blocking the sun it was nearly dark in the camp.

Danny paused a few yards from the gap he'd cut in the outer wall. A human corpse along with the bodies of a couple beastmen were lying in the dirt. The human had no eyes and didn't look like one of the half-breed guards. Where the hell had he come from? No slave ever wore a tunic that nice.

He shook his head and darted through the gap. A dead man didn't overly interest him. Putting more distance between himself and the ether pool, on the other hand, interested him a great deal.

Danny managed half a mile before a violent tremor shook the ground. A moment later an especially powerful ripple ran through the ether.

He spun in time to watch a blueish pillar shoot into the sky, obliterating the entire mountain along with the mine camp and everything else within a couple hundred yards. When the light faded, only a wasteland remained.

Danny blew out a breath. Definitely a good thing they got the beastfolk to safety before that happened.

As far as he could tell, the danger was past. Before resuming his journey, Danny flooded his body with holy energy, washing away his bumps and bruises. That done, he closed his eyes and sent his vision soaring. He needed to find Briggs and the others, hopefully before full darkness arrived.

Lucky for him he spotted a trickle of smoke only minutes after starting his search. They'd only managed about five miles before making camp. Not great, but everyone was no doubt wiped out after the escape. They couldn't have much for food. Best see if he could kill a deer or boar on his way to join them.

While Danny would usually never hunt this way, he focused his will on the nearest animal and let the magic guide his invisible eyes. Soon enough he spotted a large boar about a mile from his current position. A shot of lightning stopped its heart.

Danny marked the location of the beastfolk camp and the boar then ended his spell and set out.

It took fifteen minutes to reach the boar. During the walk, he couldn't help noticing how silent the forest was. It felt like every animal had fled. Probably an effect of the ethereal explosion. He'd read somewhere that certain animals could be sensitive to surges in ethereal activity. Hopefully he didn't disrupt the local ecology too much.

Gutting the boar took longer than he'd hoped and when he set out again it was approaching full dark. He summoned a light and followed his ethereal marker toward the waiting beastfolk.

Danny made no effort at stealth. After all they'd been through, the last thing he wanted to do was scare anyone. He thrashed through the brush as he approached the campsite and when he finally pushed through found the beastfolk spread out around the fire lying down or sitting, generally looking exhausted.

Briggs waved and hurried over. "Grimshadow said you were coming. When I saw that explosion, I was worried. What happened?"

"A lot. Let's start the boar I killed cooking and I'll tell you about it."

They'd barely gotten the boar out of storage when a beastwoman came over to join them.

"Ronin, this is my mom, Darla. Mom, this is my friend Ronin."

Danny nodded. "Pleasure, ma'am. I apologize for not speaking to you earlier, but things were a bit hectic."

She smiled. "They certainly were. Thank you for looking after my son. I can't begin to tell you how relieved I was when I saw him safe and sound."

"I didn't do that much. Briggs has been a fine companion. I'm sure everyone's hungry. We'd best get this meat cooking."

They ended up cutting the meat into strips, threading them onto sticks, and setting them up near the fire. Every eye in the place was locked on the sizzling meat. Knowing beastfolk's preferences, Danny doubted they'd wait very long before digging in.

"So what happened?" Briggs asked.

Danny shared his story. There was nothing especially secret about his project to destroy the ether pools so he left nothing out.

"Anyway, it worked. My guess is the explosion caused a chain reaction that made all the ether crystals in the mine explode. The ones I took from the storeroom might be all that are left. Around here anyway. At a minimum there shouldn't be much need for miners. What about you? I noticed a dead guy with no eyes on my way out. He wasn't a guard."

"No," Briggs said. "He was really strong. I don't think I came that close to dying even when I fought the demon bear."

Briggs recounted the fight and their escape from the camp. Danny had never heard of someone fighting by controlling their sword with magic. It was an interesting idea and he resolved to give it a try eventually.

"Everyone was exhausted so we made camp closer than I wanted to. I'm glad we got far enough away. What happens now?"

"Food and sleep for now," Danny said. "We'll take a roundabout way to the outpost where I left Val and the other beastfolk. They should still be there given the poor weather. Once you're reunited, what you do next is your decision. As for me, I've got nineteen more ether pools to find and destroy."

○

As Danny expected, the hungry beastfolk stripped the boar down to the bone before passing out. Now they sprawled around the clearing sleeping like the dead. None of them had offered to take a turn on watch, which, given how obviously exhausted they were was probably a good thing anyway. Danny planned to set a ward before he went to sleep, but he had one thing to do first.

Shifting his focus to the dagger resting beside Briggs he whispered, "Grimshadow."

A moment later he found himself in the dark space the demon spirit called home. His dark form, something between a panther and a wolf, cowered like a whipped dog as Danny approached.

"Relax, I'm not mad at you."

"Then what do you want?" Grimshadow asked.

"Tell me more about the eyeless swordsman you and Briggs fought."

"What more can I tell you? He was strong, fast, and skilled. Only his arrogance allowed us to win."

Danny frowned. "You're telling me you absorbed none of

his memories and knowledge along with his life force? I find that difficult to believe. It would be… unfortunate, if you decided to keep secrets from me."

"Well, it is possible I picked up a few choice tidbits during our brief contact. Less than I normally would, given the human's magical protections."

"That's better. Out of curiosity, why bother lying to me in the first place?"

"I'm a demon. Lying, corrupting, killing, and keeping secrets is what we do. It's an instinct."

"An unhealthy one in this case. Now talk."

"It turns out the human, his name was Nash Veil if it matters, was part of a larger group. He came to the mine to collect ether crystals they needed for a magical ritual."

Danny disliked the sound of that. "Did you get any details about the ritual?"

"Not many." Danny glared at the demon. "I swear! He was remarkably disinterested in the details of what the group was doing. The only thing that interested him was death and causing as much of it as possible. Not an unusual attitude for an Astaroth worshipper. Much as I hate them, the demon in me can't help but approve."

Danny shook his head. Heaven's mercy, he hated dealing with demons. "The details you did learn?"

"Right. The group's priest planned to raise an army of the dead. Apparently he did something to alter the plague to make it curse everyone who died of it. If they weren't blessed by a priest before they were buried or burned, their spirits would linger so they could rise again as disembodied undead. Those are the hardest kind to kill."

"That's a problem. Hopefully preventing him from getting the crystals will be enough to stop that from happen-

172

ing. Or at least delay it long enough for me to warn the temple. If they can belatedly bless the dead that should remove the threat. Where can I find these clowns?"

"The group works out of a fortress a day's run from here to the west. There are only three left: another warrior named Berend, a wizard named Voss, and the leader, a priest of Astaroth named Zane. That's all I've got, I swear."

Berend! Danny had been wondering where the traitorous assistant guild master ended up. When he killed the man this time, he'd be sure to do so in a way that didn't let him come back to life.

Given the hatred between the Reaper and Astaroth, Danny figured Grimshadow was telling him the truth. "Thanks."

Danny returned his mind to his body and considered his options. He'd never be closer to the target than he was now. Putting an end to these demon worshippers might stop a lot of future trouble before it started. Realistically, he'd be looking at a three-day detour. Not a huge deal in the grand scheme of things but a potentially huge payoff. His main worry was leaving the beastfolk to their own devices. If a large force of slave hunters tried to capture them, it might be more than Briggs could handle on his own.

Best to sleep on it and decide in the morning. Danny cast a ward around the camp, pulled his bedroll out of storage, and settled down to rest.

CHAPTER 25

Zane sat cross-legged on the floor of his makeshift temple and let his spirit mingle with the corrupt ether. He'd sacrificed enough people at this point to fully darken the ether, rendering his magic stronger than normal. He breathed in the darkness, making it a part of him. Some might say he was wasting his time, but until Nash returned with the crystals, there was nothing for Zane to do. Though relatively strong as hellpriests went, he wasn't even close to powerful enough to activate the cursed spirits he'd created without help.

As he meditated, a powerful ripple ran through the ether. It washed over him with a nearly physical presence. He'd never felt anything like it. Even worse, the ripple had come from the general direction of the mine. He had a bad feeling about it.

As if summoned by that feeling, he sensed the malevolent presence of his demonic agent. The imp wouldn't make contact without a good reason. Zane didn't believe in coincidences, especially when magic was involved.

He opened himself to the imp's presence and asked, "What is it?"

"Another of your followers has arrived in the master's hell."

"What happened?"

"How should I know?" the imp said. "As soon as his soul appeared it was absorbed. I didn't have time to question it. You should be grateful I even noticed its arrival."

"Noticing that sort of thing is your only job. If you'd failed to do so, what use would you be? In any case, I appreciate the message. Well done."

Zane severed the link and separated himself from the ether. Nash's death meant he wouldn't be bringing the crystals. He needed to send Berend at once, before whoever killed Nash could interfere further.

A few strides carried him to the stairs up to the main part of the keep. He was halfway to the top when Voss appeared, panting for breath. Zane couldn't imagine what might get the wizard moving so quickly, but doubted it would be anything good.

"Something wrong, Voss?" Zane asked.

"Did you feel it? The ripple?"

"Of course. Anyone even vaguely connected to the ether would have no trouble noticing such a thing. Do you know what it was?"

"You won't believe it. Come to the scrying chamber and see for yourself. It's... something."

Zane had never seen Voss this worked up about anything. He fell in beside the white-robed wizard and the pair hurried through the dark corridors to the scrying chamber, really just an unused room with a crystal ball.

"Have you seen Berend?" Zane asked as they walked.

"Yes. I just finished fitting him with my new bone armor. The adjustments took longer than I expected, but it's fully functional now."

"And is Berend still fully functional?"

"Of course he is," Voss said, his tone pained. For an amoral psychopath, Voss was easily upset by any perceived criticism. "I only poked a few holes in him. He's a demon, it would take way more than that to do any permanent damage."

"I'm very much reassured. Where did you leave him?"

"He went to the training yard to try the armor out. He's hoping for a sparring match when Nash gets back."

Zane grimaced. "Then he's going to be disappointed. I received word from one of my agents in the master's hell. Nash was killed not too long ago."

"You're kidding. No, never mind, you never kid. I didn't think there was anyone this side of Discourt strong enough to have a chance against Nash, much less kill him. Not counting Berend of course. Will you summon him back?"

"I can't. Nash didn't make a deal with the master. His soul has already been absorbed into the fabric of Hell."

They rounded a corner and Voss stopped outside the door of the scrying room. "If he didn't want to become a demon, why join us?"

"Nash liked killing but lacked purpose. I provided him the latter while giving him the opportunity to do the former. He didn't care much for life and sought death at the hands of a strong warrior. Perhaps I should be happy for him since it seems he got what he wanted, but mostly I'm annoyed that he's made my life more difficult."

"I didn't realize he was an idiot as well as a great swordsman." Voss shrugged and pushed the door open. "I left the crystal ball locked on the target. Take a look."

Zane walked over to the head-sized crystal ball and peered into its depths. The image was distorted, but it clearly showed a huge hole in the ground. Aside from the size, Zane couldn't see anything especially remarkable about it.

"This is what got you so excited, a hole?"

Voss gestured and the image pulled back to reveal the surrounding landscape. Zane immediately recognized the location as the mine.

"Are you excited now?" Voss asked.

"What happened?" Zane asked.

"I don't know, but the mine was the source of that ethereal wave. I traced it back and found the crater. My best guess is that all the ether crystals exploded in a chain reaction. How that might happen I couldn't begin to say."

"The loss of our ether crystals is a problem. Without a source of focused ether, I can't raise the army."

"Can't you create your own?" Voss asked.

"If I did nothing else for a year, perhaps I could collect and corrupt enough ether." Zane tapped his chin with his index finger. "We don't have any other pressing business. Wait. There might be some crystals left at the merchants' warehouse. If there was no damage to the town, it means only the local crystals exploded, right?"

Voss went over to the crystal ball and gestured again. "The town is completely unharmed. Looks like your theory is correct. Will you send Berend to collect them?"

"I'll send you both. Your pocket dimension is the safest way to transport a large quantity of crystals."

Voss scowled. "I hate fieldwork."

"So you've told me on numerous occasions. Happily, I

don't need you to like the job. Just do it. Bring back every crystal they have, even the inferior ones. With the mine destroyed, their value has become nearly priceless."

"Fine. I need to change into my work clothes."

"I'll speak to Berend. Meet us in the courtyard when you're ready. And don't delay. I want this finished sooner rather than later."

Zane didn't hear whatever Voss muttered as he stalked out of the scrying room but doubted it was complimentary. Let him complain as much as he wanted to as long as he did as he was told. Valuable as he was, even Voss could be replaced should it be necessary.

Putting his shut-in wizard out of his mind, Zane headed for the courtyard. A demon spirit brushed past him as he walked down the hall. There were a handful of the invisible creatures wandering the fortress doing odd jobs, mostly cleaning and making sure no vermin got in to damage their books. They had no real personality or will and were so weak they'd barely be suitable for animating a zombie. On the plus side they were easy to summon and took no effort to maintain in this reality.

Zane passed through the front door and strode out into the courtyard where Berend was doing sword forms with the new Hell-forged black iron blade Zane had given him. His body was encased in thick white bone from head to toe. Voss's new armor left a great deal to be desired in terms of subtlety, but in a battle it would no doubt strike terror into the hearts of anyone seeing it and that wasn't a bad thing.

Berend spotted him and stopped his practice. "When's Nash getting back? I want to give this armor a proper test."

"Nash is dead and the mine destroyed."

"What happened?"

Zane shrugged. "No idea. You know Nash didn't want to return. His soul is already gone and his body was likely destroyed in the explosion. I'm sending you and Voss to Crystal Veil's warehouse to collect all their in-stock crystals. Hopefully there will be enough to complete the ritual."

Berend flashed his fangs. "I'd rather go alone. Voss will complain nonstop."

"I have no doubt. In fact, he's already begun, but his pocket dimension is the safest way to transport the crystals. With the mine gone, finding more will be no easy task. We can't risk this bunch getting destroyed."

"The merchants are unlikely to just hand their goods over."

"I'm confident you and Voss will be able to convince them." Zane sensed a presence and turned to watch as Voss emerged from the fortress for the first time in probably five years.

The wizard had swapped his white robes for dark trousers and a matching tunic and cloak. He carried his bone staff in his right hand and had his pale face twisted up in a scowl. "Let's get this over with. The sooner I can return to my research, the better."

"That's the spirit," Zane said. "Berend, don't forget your illusion amulet."

Berend pulled the amulet out of his pocket and slipped it over his head. The air shimmered around him and he once more looked like a normal man. The two of them hit the road without another word. Given Voss's physical limitations, it would likely take them three days to reach the town then another three back.

Zane swallowed a sigh. It wasn't ideal, but if this didn't work, he was going to have to abandon the project altogether. Not at all an appealing prospect given the amount of time he'd dedicated to it.

Well, he'd just have to think positive. Despite their personality quirks, Berend and Voss were both alpha elite adventurers. This task should be simple for them.

He smiled at his foolishness. Nothing had been simple since he started this project and Zane doubted that was going to change anytime soon.

CHAPTER 26

Despite being the last one to go to sleep, Danny was the first to wake. Nothing troubled the camp during the night. As he expected, no normal animals would approach such a large group. While he had a free moment, Danny dug out his map and did a quick calculation as to how far the group would need to go to rejoin Val and the other beastfolk he'd rescued at the elf-blood outpost. Avoiding the roads would be a necessity, especially in this part of the world. Given the speed the former slaves could manage, he figured they'd need a month minimum and likely six weeks.

That was a long time to keep such a large group together, safe, and fed. It was a lucky thing that this world was a lot less densely populated than Earth. The worst of the winter weather had passed, which would help, but it was still going to be a major undertaking. Spending a few days gathering supplies before they set out wouldn't be a terrible idea.

That said, Danny wanted to get everyone further away

from the lake communities. Staying this close to their former owners was just asking for trouble.

But first, breakfast. He sent his awareness soaring out in search of a large animal. Everything he'd seen indicated beastfolk were primarily carnivorous. Cornmeal pancakes would doubtless be looked on poorly. There were a few humans in the group. He'd make enough for himself and them to go with the meat. No one had complained about just meat last night, but they were starving and anything was better than nothing.

Fortunately, it didn't take long to find a deer and zap it with lightning. He marked its location with an ethereal beacon and opened his eyes. The beastfolk were finally stirring, though Briggs remained sound asleep. His mother, luckily, was awake and rubbing the sleep from her eyes.

Danny walked over and crouched beside her. "Morning. I killed a deer a moment ago. Could you let Briggs know where I went? I shouldn't be long and when I return I can start breakfast."

Darla turned a fond gaze on her son and said, "After the fight yesterday he'll likely still be asleep when you come back. We'll start a fire. Though they may be too nervous to say it, everyone is grateful for all you've done for us."

"I'm glad I was able to help. If you'll excuse me." Danny stood and hurried to retrieve his kill.

The walking was easy and ten minutes after he set out, he reached the deer. It was kind of scrawny after the winter, but meat was meat. He gutted it and tossed the carcass into storage. Half an hour later he reached the group's camp.

True to her word, Darla had a fire started. When he gave them the deer, she and several other women got busy cutting it up. It seemed fixing breakfast wouldn't be his responsibility after all. He'd make the pancakes later.

"Ronin."

He turned to find Briggs up and moving around. The kid didn't look much worse for the wear. "How are you feeling?"

"A little sore but otherwise fine. A good night's sleep did wonders, not to mention all that tasty meat. What's the plan for today?"

"I need to make a side trip, but first I want to move you guys somewhere a little more remote, hopefully where you won't run into any humans. While I'm gone, I'm hoping you and the hunters can stock up on meat. There's plenty of game in this forest, but I know this isn't the sort of place you're used to hunting."

Briggs patted his sheathed blade. "I can always find game with Grimshadow's magic. Where are you going?"

"To deal with the ones ultimately responsible for both the plague and your capture. Shouldn't take me more than three or four days. I figure everyone could use a little more time to rest and recover. If things go badly, you'll have to find your own way back."

"It won't. No one can beat you."

Danny grinned. While he appreciated Briggs's confidence, he was far from invincible. Still, Danny wouldn't go down to just anyone. Whatever the risk, it was worth it to deal with the hellpriest. With him gone, the odds of the plague victims rising again dropped to nearly zero.

Not to mention, leaving loose ends behind was just asking for trouble.

⟁

Danny frowned at the dark stone fortress. He hadn't had any trouble finding the place; it oozed corruption like a weeping boil oozed puss. The main keep was three stories aboveground and who knew how many below. Why someone built a fortress this deep in the wilderness was another question. Maybe it just seemed like a good place to do shady business.

He'd gotten the beastfolk set up in a nice little valley beside a partially frozen stream. At minimum they'd have plenty of water and he was confident Briggs could keep them fed and hopefully stock up on enough meat to last for the rest of their trip. The humans had decided to part ways with the group, so they wouldn't need anything else for food.

But that wasn't his problem. Danny needed to focus on what was waiting inside. There were probably demons and undead guards at a minimum, though none were visible outside. They shouldn't be a major issue. Berend reborn as a demon, on the other hand, was another matter. Especially if he had two magic users backing him up.

Danny took the ethersword out of storage and strode forward. He didn't bother with a stealth field. Getting the enemy to come to him would be more convenient. Unfortunately, nothing came charging out of the fortress to try and kill him.

He paused outside the huge double doors, but sensed nothing from beyond them aside from the ambient corruption. There could be a whole army in there for all he could tell.

Three quick slashes created an opening the size of a normal door. He strode through the opening into a rather empty and gloomy entryway. He didn't have a second to appreciate the depressing decor before a shadowy presence defined by glowing red eyes surged out at him from deeper in the keep.

Danny punched it with the mithril hilt and, as he hoped, the demon spirit vanished in a puff of corrupt vapor. It was far easier to purify bodiless spirits like that than try to cut them apart with the blade.

A few seconds passed but nothing else attacked him. He doubted that spirit was the only occupant of this fortress. Since he couldn't sense anything, his only option was a room-by-room search, his least favorite thing to do going all the way back to basic training.

But that was the job so best to get on with it.

A set of steps at the rear of the entry hall went to the second floor and a doorway to his right led deeper into the keep. Since he had no desire to end up sandwiched between enemies above and below, he went for the doorway.

The dark hallway led nowhere in particular. Fifteen paces further in he found the first door. Of course it was closed and locked. The ethersword made short work of that and he kicked it open. Crates of supplies, mostly crystals, vials, and other items useful for working with magic, were stacked up in random piles that Danny doubted would stand up to a light breeze. His old quartermaster would've hit the roof if he saw the back room at the commissary in this kind of shape.

Danny shook his head and moved on. At the next intersection he turned left and froze. Coming from the opposite direction was a surprisingly handsome fellow with pale skin dressed in a dark robe and surrounded by dozens of undead. A demonic skull decorated the front of his robe.

The two of them stared at each other for a moment before the man said, "Kill him!"

The undead surged forward.

Danny activated his physical enhancements and rushed to meet them.

The ethersword sliced through their undead flesh with comical ease and in less than ten seconds all the monsters were reduced to twitching lumps of flesh. The hellpriest, at least Danny assumed that's what the man was, had vanished.

He hurried down the hall and found himself facing a set of stairs leading to the basement. Of course, that was the perfect place for a demon worshipper to keep his lair. Avius had his lab in the basement as well. Was it an evil magic user thing? Surely there had to be at least one demon-worshipping plague merchant that liked fresh air and sunshine.

He swallowed a sigh and slowly descended, every sense alert for traps. He reached the bottom with no issues and found himself in a weird, makeshift temple. The priest was standing behind a black altar, glaring at Danny for all he was worth. Up close he looked younger than you'd expect for a hellpriest. Why Danny thought hellpriests should look like withered old men was another question.

"You've come a long way to die," the priest said.

"Unless you've got something more dangerous around here than those pitiful zombies, I'm not overly concerned. I assume you're Zane, the priest of Astaroth." Danny stalked closer, taking his time and making sure he didn't stumble into anything.

"How do you know my name?"

"Nash was kind enough to provide it. I expected to find Berend and Voss here as well. Are they hiding somewhere else?"

"Did you kill Nash?"

"Don't you know it's rude to answer a question with a question?"

Zane snarled and threw his hand forward.

Dark flames surged at Danny.

He punched the ethersword's hilt toward them, the mithril purifying the corruption and snuffing them out.

Zane stared, mouth partway open, as the last wisps of his spell faded away.

"You're not the first wielder of corrupt ether I've fought. Nothing like a bit of mithril to deal with that sort of thing."

Zane looked left and right, fear and desperation twisting his face. "Surely we can make a deal. My master is most generous with those who serve him."

Danny shook his head. "Not interested. If you tell me where to find Voss and Berend, I'll make this quick."

Zane straightened, seeming to have found his courage. "Even if you kill me, I'll be reborn in the master's hell as a demon. You'll get no satisfaction from me."

"I like your optimism. You think Astaroth will reward you after you failed to raise your plague army? I've got my doubts, but maybe. One way to find out for sure."

Danny leapt the altar and swung his fist with all his might. The mithril hilt struck a dark barrier, shattered it, and crashed into Zane's head, reducing it to pulp. The priest's body crashed to the floor, never to rise again.

With a grimace, Danny burned the blood and brains off his hand. He didn't like killing people that way, but using the mithril directly ensured Zane's soul was purified and wouldn't be reborn in Hell. At least that was how it worked with demons, hopefully hellpriests were the same. Danny was willing to deal with the mess to avoid that.

"Okay, that was easier than I expected." Danny spun in a

slow circle, taking in the temple slash torture chamber. The place was a mess with bloodstains on the floor and all sorts of torture devices here and there. He could almost feel the echo of pain in the air.

Unfortunately he couldn't do anything about it. Purifying this place was a job for a priest. The best Danny could do was collect all the evil stuff and lock it up in storage where it couldn't do any harm. So he got to work. First he patted down Zane's body and removed a ring and an amulet that did heaven knew what. Next anything even remotely valuable looking went in. When he finished with the basement, Danny went upstairs and continued his work.

He went room to room gathering everything of value, destroying a few more demon spirits and undead in the process. The biggest prize as far as he was concerned was a hundred-plus leather-bound tomes that made up the group's modest library. He had no idea what sort of knowledge they held but doubted it was the sort of intel you'd want to leave lying around.

When he finished scouring the place from top to bottom, he strode back out the hole he'd cut in the main gate. Cleanup had taken most of the day and the sun was about to set. Not the best time to be traveling, but he didn't especially want to hang around this wretched place. The forest at night would be far more pleasant.

As for Berend and Voss, Danny had no idea where to find them. Which was a shame as he'd much prefer to finish off the whole group, but it was what it was. He needed to return to Briggs and the other beastfolk. Their reunion with Val and the others had been delayed long enough.

CHAPTER 27

The merchants at Crystal Veil Trading had been every bit as reluctant to give up their remaining stock of ether crystals as Berend had expected, but after he killed all the warehouse guards they decided to do the right thing. The number they had on hand had been disappointing and the less said about the quality the better. He had serious doubts they would be enough to do what Zane needed, but at the end of the day they couldn't conjure crystals out of thin air so these would have to do.

Berend flicked a glance at his traveling companion. Voss hadn't so much as lifted a finger on the mission so far. All he did was open and close his personal pocket dimension while glowering at everyone. He also hadn't complained, so that was a plus. If Voss liked one thing almost as much as fiddling with magical odds and ends, it was complaining. He and the late Nash had that in common.

But whatever, they were nearly back to headquarters, mission completed with nary a hiccup.

Berend strode another ten paces before he realized Voss

had stopped, his head cocked as if hearing something inaudible to anyone else.

"What?" Berend asked.

"Something's wrong. At this range I should be able to sense the demon spirits bound to the fortress, but they're gone."

"Maybe Zane has them doing something." Berend knew absolutely nothing about how binding magic worked, but it didn't seem unreasonable.

"No, the demons are bound to the fortress. He couldn't send them off on an errand without breaking that bond. If Zane needed a demon spirit for something else, he'd just summon a new one. No, something is definitely wrong."

"Then maybe stop standing there and hurry up. We're less than a mile away."

To Berend's considerable surprise, Voss picked up his pace. That more than anything he said convinced him there was a problem. Voss and hurrying were not well acquainted.

Fifteen minutes later they reached the clearing surrounding their fortress and Berend confirmed with his own eyes that there was, indeed, a problem. Someone had cut a hole in the main gate. Those doors were made of ten-inch-thick solid oak boards. An ogre with an ax wouldn't be able to cut through them in half a day.

When they reached the entrance Berend ran a finger along the smooth end of the severed boards. He had no idea what sort of weapon would make a cut like that, but it had to be magic. He glanced at Voss, but the wizard made no move to enter first. Because of course he didn't, miserable coward.

Berend drew his sword and stepped through the opening. The entry area looked the same as always. He glanced toward the stairs but turned down the hall instead. If Zane was anywhere, the basement was most likely.

Voss followed along behind him. When they reached the storeroom Berend paused and looked inside. It was empty.

"We've been robbed," Voss said. "Do you think this is how monsters felt when we raided their lairs?"

"There were never any left alive when we raided their lairs. Come on." Berend was pretty sure no dangers lingered in the fortress, but he didn't put his sword away just in case he was wrong. He assumed living men had done this, but if it was a rival cult, their corruption would be as hard to detect as any other.

They reached the basement stairs and climbed down. Like with the storeroom above, everything had been taken. Well, everything except Zane's headless body. That lay in a puddle of blood beside Astaroth's altar.

Voss hurried over and knelt beside the body. He held out a hand and dark energy swirled around it before shooting into Zane's body. Since it was pretty obvious what killed him, Berend assumed he was trying to learn something else.

At last Voss stood. "He was killed by some sort of holy magic. His essence has been purified. It's possible he won't be reborn in Astaroth's hell."

"What sort of holy magic?" Berend asked.

"No way to tell. I can only see the aftermath, not the cause. But only holy magic of some sort would do this. What are we going to do now?"

That was a good question. As a demon, Berend had no hope of finding a place in civilized society. He could join another cult of Astaroth, but then he was apt to end up serving a priest even more obnoxious than Zane. That didn't appeal to him at all.

"I figure we've got two options. Go our own way and find some new project, or hunt down the ones responsible for this insult and make them pay."

"Even if we wanted to get revenge, we don't know who did it," Voss said.

"I can make a pretty good guess. Likely those knights I fought figured out some way to track me back here and when they found Zane instead, well, you can imagine what a bunch of Branik worshippers would do with a priest of Astaroth. Zane never was worth a damn in a fight."

"Hunting down a bunch of holy knights doesn't appeal to me," Voss said.

"Why don't you go check the library? I'll wager what you find will change your mind."

Voss's eyes nearly bugged out of his face and he hurried past Berend back up the stairs. Berend followed along behind at a more sedate pace, a little smile playing about his lips. Sometimes it was almost too easy.

He found Voss upstairs, staring at the empty shelves. As Berend had expected, all the books were gone.

"Those bastards stole my entire library. They're not going to get away with it."

"Do you have some way to find them?" Berend asked.

"That will be tricky. I can try and scry for the books, but I don't know what the knights look like well enough to search for them."

"Can you look in my mind and take the memory of our fight?"

Voss frowned. "You trust me to poke around inside your head?"

Berend chuckled. "It's not in your best interest to do anything which might make me less able to keep the knights from reaching you. I trust you to the extent our interests align. So will it work?"

Voss nodded. "It should. But I need to ready a scrying vessel. I doubt they left the crystal ball behind. I'll need a few days at least to prepare. The lack of material will make it more difficult, but not impossible."

"Good. Is there anything I can do to speed the process?"

"No, but you could check the larder. Unlike you, I still need to eat. If the knights cleared that out as well, you'll need to go hunting."

Berend nodded. "I'll handle the food situation. You focus on finding the thieves."

Voss nodded and strode out of the library.

Berend hated leaving enemies alive and this was why. On the plus side, it looked like he'd have a chance to remedy his error.

CHAPTER 28

Father Koen sat at the head of an oval table in the Temple of the Goddess's meeting room. With him were high-ranking members of the other faiths in Discourt. They were meeting to finalize plans for the healing caravan. Mother Ankie had asked him to take charge of the project and, much as he disliked the idea of leaving the city for an extended period, he understood her reasoning. He had the most experience planning large-scale projects, so it made sense for him to handle it.

He turned to Father Kinlet, a brawny member of Branik's church who was in charge of the caravan's security. "Are the knights prepared?"

"Rest assured, Father Koen, our elite knights will be ready to ride as soon as the caravan is set." He heaved a sigh. "I wish they'd succeeded in killing the demon. Knowing it's out there getting up to heaven knows what mischief worries me."

"I'm sure they did their best. According to the report I read, the demon fled by air. There's little mortal men can do when faced with a foe who can fly."

Father Kinlet grunted, seeming little reassured. Father Koen knew how he felt. Demons were a scourge on the world. Destroying them wherever they hid was the duty of all holy warriors. Of course, knowing your duty and being capable of carrying it out were two different things.

He turned to Adonael's representative. "Have you sent warnings to your sister temples?"

The priestess nodded. "We contacted all the larger temples, who will branch out and inform the smaller village temples. Everyone should be on alert by the end of spring."

"Excellent," Father Koen said. "As for us, everyone in the city has completed the immunity ritual and Mother Ankie has confirmed that there are no more afflicted people. The caravan will be ready to depart in the morning. We'll be heading east down the trade road to the heart of the most heavily affected area. If there's nothing else, I'll adjourn the meeting."

Both of his companions shook their heads, so he stood and clapped once. "Meeting adjourned. Father Kinlet, I'll see you and the knights at first light."

The meeting broke up and Father Koen escorted his guests to the front door. When they'd gone he turned back and jumped half a foot when he found Avius standing silently waiting for him.

"I'm going to put a bell on you. What is it?"

"I detected magical scrying directed this way. Not at the temple specifically, but Discourt in general. I don't know if it's relevant, but with the caravan leaving tomorrow, I thought it best to warn you."

Father Koen scrubbed a hand across his weary face. He needed another problem like he needed a hole in the head. "Could you find the source?"

"Only that it was coming from the northwest and a fair distance away. I lack the necessary equipment for anything more precise."

"We're going east, so hopefully whatever it was it won't affect us. But I will warn Father Kinlet to be especially vigilant. Thank you for the warning."

Avius offered a polite bow. Whatever Father Koen had thought of the man when he first arrived at the temple—and it hadn't been good—he couldn't deny the wizard had been a helpful member of the team, doing nothing even vaguely problematic. Perhaps he truly had turned over a new leaf. Stranger things had happened and with the Goddess's grace all things were possible.

Father Koen would offer his prayers tonight and whatever happened tomorrow, he'd deal with it then.

Berend stared at the back of Voss's head as the wizard peered into a shallow basin of water. Unlike with the crystal ball, no image appeared on the smooth surface so he couldn't see what Voss saw. It was annoying, but given their limited resources it was a wonder he'd found a way to activate a long-range scrying spell in the first place.

He shifted, took a step to pace around the scrying chamber, then caught himself. Distractions would not be welcome right now. Berend hadn't killed anyone in far too long and his demonic nature was starting to flare up. If he didn't find an enemy to murder, Voss might be in trouble.

A shudder ran through the wizard and he looked away from the water. "I found them."

Berend flashed his fangs. "Excellent! How far away are they?"

"They're a day outside of Discourt, heading east, apparently on caravan guard duty." Voss rubbed his bloodshot eyes and focused on Berend. "You know what that means, right?"

Berend's pleasure withered. "They didn't raid the fortress and kill Zane."

"Correct. Unless they had access to teleportation or portal magic, which would've left signs that I didn't find, there's no way they could've attacked us and made it all the way back to Discourt in the few days that passed. Whoever killed Zane and took our supplies, it wasn't them."

Berend cursed long and loud. "Any suggestions for how we find whoever did raid the fortress?"

Voss shook his head. "Loath as I am to say this, I think the time has come for us to accept our situation and move on. My library can be rebuilt and our skills are such that finding employment shouldn't be an issue. Perhaps we could go back to being adventurers."

"We've been banned by the guild," Berend said. "We'd have to take jobs without their support, a tricky prospect at the best of times. And working for a different cult of Astaroth doesn't appeal to me either. Some arrogant priest is liable to try and control me, which will lead to me killing him and becoming an enemy of the cult. No, I don't like that idea."

"So, what then?" Voss asked. "Sitting around here twiddling my thumbs doesn't appeal to me."

Berend smiled as an idea came to him. "You want access to books and magic, right? What if we killed the Reaper's followers in Elfhome and claimed the city for ourselves? Imagine the power you could find there. We could set up a new cult of Astaroth with ourselves at the top. The master would be well pleased to have servants of his rival slaughtered."

Berend watched as fear and greed warred on Voss's face. When it came to magic and secrets, Elfhome was the crown jewel. Any ambitious wizard would want access. With his new power, backed up by Voss's magic, they could take down whatever guardians protected the place. And if they failed, a prospect Berend considered unlikely, it would be better to die in an all-or-nothing gamble than to rot in obscurity.

"Agreed," Voss said at last. "I know Avius tried to enter and failed. Overcoming an obstacle that turned such a brilliant wizard aside appeals to me. Gaining access to the secrets of the half-elves would make me the most powerful wizard in the area if not the world. That's worth a gamble."

"Then let's go."

CHAPTER 29

R iko flew around above the forest surrounding Elfhome, making sure to keep herself invisible to avoid anyone spotting her from a distance. Not that they could do anything even if they did see her, but the training from her life as a Daughter of the Reaper made stealth second nature. Though she disliked admitting it, she missed Daniel. It was nice having someone to talk to other than an ill-tempered imp and a book-obsessed librarian. He'd treated her like a person rather than a monster which came as a surprise. Most people were less than kind to demons.

Given that, it was rather unkind of her to hope he ran into trouble on his mission so he'd have to return and do more research. She smiled and banked right. At least the view here was prettier than the skies over Black City. The bleak hellscape of the master's home left something to be desired in terms of looks.

She was about to fly over another part of the forest when she felt one of the guardian demons die. A quick snap of her wings sent Riko diving toward the city. There weren't many people capable of defeating even weak demons and the guardians, while low on the demonic power scale, were still pretty strong. Whoever was approaching could not be taken lightly.

As soon as she landed, the imp who served as her assistant came hopping over. It was easy to see why Briggs had named it Toad. The ugly, green-scaled thing did look a great deal like a giant toad.

"What's going on?" Riko asked.

"A human and a demon entered the forest fifteen minutes ago. They encountered and defeated the nearest guardian. They're headed straight toward us."

"I assume the demon isn't one of the master's."

"No, the magical signature indicates Astaroth. Weird there're no undead with them. What do you want to do?"

"Have all the guardians in that section converge on the pair. I need to prepare for their arrival."

"There are six guardians in the area. You don't think that will be enough?" Toad asked.

"If it is, I'll be happy to be wrong. If it's not, I want to be ready. Send the order." Riko left Toad to carry out his task and made her way to the temple. She left her sword on the altar when not expecting a fight so it could soak up the master's corruption. That would be helpful against the human, though the demon wouldn't be overly troubled by a little extra corruption.

She barely entered the altar chamber when the master's awareness settled over her. *You will need help to deal with this enemy. I will summon Grimshadow's bearer and ask him to bring Daniel.*

To have the Reaper state outright that he doubted she

could defeat the approaching threat left her stunned, but only for a moment. "I'll hold them off as long as I can, Master."

She strode over to the altar, snatched her sword off the top, and strapped it to her back. Riko closed her eyes and asked for the Reaper's blessing.

Dark power flooded into her, making her hair stand on end for a moment. "I won't fail you, Master."

So saying she turned and strode out. If the enemy was as powerful as the master thought, she hoped Daniel and Briggs arrived quickly. Though her death would only be temporary, she had no desire to experience it a second time.

Toad was waiting for her in the central clearing. "They're tearing through the guardians as quickly as they show up. What did we do to piss off Astaroth's cult?"

"What makes you think we had to do anything in particular? The master hates Astaroth and the feeling is, I'm sure, mutual. I'm frankly surprised this sort of thing doesn't happen more often."

"Think you can take them?" Toad asked.

"The Master doesn't. He's calling Briggs and Daniel in for backup. I hope they get here before the enemy."

"That makes two of us. If this thing kills you, I won't be far behind."

"Your concern warms my heart."

With nothing to do but wait, Riko paced and opened her awareness to fully take in the surrounding area. She soon sensed the approaching demon. It was like a black flame burning up everything in its path. She'd never felt anything quite like it. The demon's human companion was a far dimmer presence. Given the difference in their power, she couldn't help wondering which was the master and which the servant.

Not that it mattered. Both were trespassing on the Reaper's territory and both would die for the insult. That was the Master's command and Riko's duty.

Far too soon a human-looking demon stepped into the city. He wore some sort of armor made from bone and carried a black iron sword in his right hand. The demon's eyes blazed red. At the edge of the forest, a man in dark robes clutched a bone-white staff.

"Are you the final defender?" the demon asked. "After all I heard about this place, I expected more. Your guardians were pathetic. Do you think you can give me a better workout?"

Riko drew her own Hell-forged blade. It crackled with the Reaper's power. "One way to find out."

The demon flashed its needle-sharp fangs.

They charged at the same instant.

Their blades came together with a horrible clash of metal on metal. Corrupt energy flew off in every direction as they battled. Riko had fought many battles but never against an enemy demon this strong.

Blow after blow, the battle raged.

Their blades locked and her opponent grinned, their faces inches apart. "I haven't had this much fun in ages."

Riko had no energy to spare for idle chatter. If he had strength to spare talking, she was in worse trouble than she thought.

A hard shove sent Riko flying back. Her wings snapped open, stabilizing her.

Her hands vibrated from the heavy blows, making it hard to hold her sword. Even worse, the wizard hadn't even gotten involved yet. She was barely holding out as it was. If he joined in, she was in real trouble.

"You're good," the demon said. "I'll give you that. But you're not nearly good enough to beat me."

Riko said nothing, but in her heart, she feared he was right. If help was coming, she hoped it got here soon.

◯

B riggs marched at the front of the ragged line of beastfolk, his scuffed boots crunching the frosty grass. Sunlight slanted through the trees, a hint of warmth heralding the arrival of spring. He breathed deep, savoring the fresh air. It was wonderful being far enough from Crystal Lake to no longer have the stink of rotting fish filling the air.

For the first time in months, he felt optimistic about his people's future. His pack was free. Scores of others were also free and they were heading east to meet up with their pack mates. Most importantly, they were now hundreds of miles from the slavers who had captured them.

All in all, things were as good as he dared hope for.

The thought had barely formed when he found himself dragged into the darkness Grimshadow called home. The demon hadn't done anything this aggressive since he first made a pact with the creature and became his bearer.

"What's going on?" Briggs asked.

Grimshadow separated himself from the darkness. He was a huge, four-legged beast with glowing red eyes that towered over Briggs. "Enemies have come to Elfhome. The Reaper requires you to come and fight."

Briggs bared his teeth. "I just freed my people from slavery, and now you want me to turn and walk into a battle that might leave them undefended? Why should I?"

"You were told there would be a price to gain my power. Time to pay up. This is not a request. The master requires your presence. He also wishes you to ask Daniel to come as well."

"Elfhome is miles from here! How are we supposed to get there in time?"

"You'll teleport. Normally my power is short range, but the Master has created a link between me and his temple. Speak to the human and be convincing."

The darkness shattered. Briggs stumbled, blinking at the sudden brightness. Ronin and his mother stood close by on either side of him, frowning with concern.

"What's wrong?" his mother asked. "You just stopped moving and stared at nothing."

Briggs shook his head to try to clear it. "Grimshadow got a message from the Reaper. Someone's attacking Elfhome and he wants us to go help deal with it."

"Us?" Ronin asked.

"You and me. Grimshadow says some special magic of the Reaper's will let us teleport to his temple. Will you help?"

Ronin nodded. "I'm quite fond of Riko. I'd hate to see anything happen to her. Plus, they did me a favor. It would hardly be honorable to ignore a call for help now."

Ronin turned to address the beastfolk, who stared at them with worried eyes. "Okay everyone, Briggs and I have to leave for a while. If you keep heading southeast, you'll stay on course. Avoid the settlements and take your time. We'll catch up to you as soon as we can."

Briggs admired the way Ronin spoke so confidently, reassuring everyone. One day he hoped to be a leader like his human friend. Though he knew that day was far away.

The hardening of the beastfolk's resolve was an almost visible thing. Their backs straightened and something glittered in their eyes. The group had been relying on Briggs and Ronin since they left the mine. This was a chance for them to see for themselves that they could survive on their own.

Briggs very much hoped they didn't come to regret obeying the Reaper's summons. Not that he had any choice in the matter.

Briggs held out his hand and Ronin grasped it in the beastfolk style. He was about to tell Grimshadow to transport them when his mother said, "Take care of yourself. I don't think I could stand to lose you a second time."

"I'll be okay, Mom. I knew there would be a price for the power I needed to free you all. Now it's time to pay. Do it!"

Grimshadow's power surged through him, stronger than anything Briggs had ever felt. And it wasn't just the demon's presence in his mind. Something darker, vaster, lurked at the edge of his perception. That had to be the demon lord.

Briggs gasped, back arching as the magic tried to tear him apart. A dark tunnel appeared around them.

They flew through a depthless abyss. Time lost all meaning. Only the firm pressure of Ronin's grip anchored Briggs to reality. Without it he feared his mind would've been lost forever.

Then it was over. Solid ground slammed into Briggs's feet and he staggered. Ronin caught him before he could fall.

Briggs blinked, disoriented, as he looked around at the dark stone and flickering light of the Reaper's temple.

He didn't even have time to ask a question before darkness swallowed him again and he passed out.

CHAPTER 30

T he creepy aura of the Reaper's temple nearly
distracted Danny so much that he missed Briggs
fainting. The kid's body went limp and his eyes
rolled back in his head. Danny barely caught him in time.
Using that much magic must've overwhelmed his system.
Hardly a shock given how far they traveled. Danny lowered
him to the floor and sighed. Whatever fighting was to be
done, he'd be doing it alone.

Daniel. The Reaper's dark voice echoed in Danny's mind.
Riko is losing her fight.

Danny clenched his jaw. Briggs would be fine here. At
least he would be as long as Danny won. Riko, on the other
hand, sounded like she was in serious trouble. With a final
glance at Briggs's unconscious figure, Danny turned toward
the exit, taking the ethersword out of storage as he did.

He sprinted out of the temple and raced up the stairs
then out into the streets of Elfhome. In a ruined plaza, Riko
was locked in vicious melee with a lean, dark swordsman
whose eyes glowed blood red. He was encased in some sort

of white armor. Danny had never seen anything quite like it.

Danny's eyes narrowed. Despite the changes, he recognized Berend. For a guy who got his head cut off, he was doing remarkably well. Off to the side, back near the edge of the forest, a dark-robed wizard watched the battle, his white staff wreathed with dark magic. That had to be Voss.

Someone must be smiling over him. He'd feared the bastards had escaped, but it looked like he was going to have another chance to wrap up the loose ends after all. A predatory smile spread across Danny's face. He wouldn't lose them this time.

A powerful blow sent Riko flying.

Before Berend could move to finish her off, Danny rushed in.

The ethersword crashed against Berend's Hell-forged black iron sword. His strike took Berend by surprise and sent him flying halfway across the courtyard.

He glanced over at Riko. She didn't look badly injured, just worn out. Her glowing red eyes were wide with surprise and relief. Danny offered her a nod of reassurance before he leapt to engage Berend.

Their swords locked, putting their faces just inches apart. Berend snarled in recognition, baring fangs in a vicious grin. "I was so hoping we'd meet again, Ronin. This time I'll be sending you to hell."

Danny grinned back. "Zane was confident too. It won't work out any better for you than it did for him."

"You raided our fortress? And here I thought those idiot knights tracked me there."

Danny'd had enough conversation. He broke the lock and sent Berend staggering back.

Berend recovered quickly and the battle was joined. The ethersword darted and slashed only to be turned aside by Berend's blade. He was easily twice as fast now, but not nearly as fast as Danny.

He pressed his advantage, the ethersword a blur of motion as he hammered at Berend's defenses, driving the demon back with each blow.

A hard slash forced Berend's sword out of line.

Danny lunged, planning to pierce whatever passed for the demon's heart.

Before the blow could land, some force picked him up and hurled him back. Out of the corner of his eye he spotted Voss, his staff leveled, ready to cast again.

Shit!

Danny backflipped, avoiding a burst of black flames by the narrowest of margins.

The moment he landed, Berend was there, sword swinging.

He turned the strike aside by a sliver, but ended up off balance and staggering back.

More blows rained down, pushing Danny's defenses to the limit. A glancing blow with the ethersword skipped off Berend's white armor.

A second blast of dark fire forced him back before he could make another swing. Berend was tough enough, but avoiding Voss's magic was making this situation impossible.

Options raced through Danny's mind, but they all sucked. He couldn't go for Voss, Berend would cut him down in a heartbeat if he turned his back. He also couldn't land a solid blow on Berend with the wizard covering for him. Worst off all, eventually even Danny would run out of stamina.

While he was thinking and dodging, the magical

bombardment just stopped. Danny risked a glance past Berend.

Briggs stood over Voss's crumpled form, the wizard's blood staining Grimshadow. The kid's eyes blazed crimson, pulsing with an unholy light. The demon had seized control of Briggs's body.

Danny grimaced but couldn't very well complain. The best thing he could do was finish Berend quickly. With Voss out of the picture, Danny could give Berend his full attention.

He rained down a whirlwind of strikes, the ethersword humming as it cut the air with blinding speed. Berend snarled but there was also fear creeping into his expression.

Danny pressed hard, not giving Berend a moment to recover.

Berend lashed out with a powerful, desperate blow, staggering Danny a step back.

Berend leapt, trying to take to the air.

Riko raised a pale hand and tendrils of darkness lashed out, ensnaring Berend and slamming him to the ground.

Danny didn't hesitate.

He lunged.

The ethersword pierced Berend's armor and burst out his back. The demon shrieked and thrashed, all signs of his former humanity long gone.

Danny ripped the blade out and smashed the mithril hilt into Berend's face over and over until he went still and stopped moving.

That had been far too close.

Breathing hard, Danny put the sword away and turned to face Briggs, whose eyes still glowed demon red. "Release him, now."

Briggs shuddered and Danny caught him before he could hit the ground. He slipped Grimshadow into the sheath at Briggs's side and turned to find Riko on her feet.

"You okay?" Danny asked.

She offered a stunning smile. "Demons heal quickly. At least assuming their skulls aren't crushed by a mithril weapon. That was rather brutal."

"Yeah, but it worked. The kid's going to need time to recover. Is it okay if I put him in the same room as before?"

"Of course, I'll open the doors for you. It's good you came when you did. I've never fought such a powerful opponent."

"Berend was a good fighter as a man. As a demon he was on another level. Having a wizard to back him up didn't hurt anything. Can you clean up the bodies? Their gear isn't the sort of thing I want getting into the wrong hands."

Her laugh was as beautiful as the rest of her. "Plenty would say my hands are the wrong hands."

Danny grinned. "Yeah, but for a demon you don't seem so bad. After I rest a bit, how about you tell me what happened? I'd also like to stop by the library."

"Now that the threat is dealt with, I'm at your disposal. When you're ready, just call my name."

Their chat had brought them to the central tower and Danny eagerly dropped Briggs off in his room before ducking into his own. A quick nap would be just the thing.

CHAPTER 31

Danny groaned and opened his eyes, his body aching from head to toe. It took him a moment to remember where he was and what happened. Right, Elfhome, the fight with Berend and Voss. No wonder he was so sore. With a grimace, he sat up and bathed his body with holy magic, letting it flow through him. The pain receded as torn muscles and bruised bones knit back together.

He rolled out of bed, stood, and stretched. Everything was working properly now. His stomach growled, reminding him he hadn't eaten anything in far too long. In the kitchen, he fried up a steak. He didn't have much in the way of supplies in his storage after so long, but a nice venison steak hit the spot.

Now to see how Briggs was doing.

Danny made the short walk down the familiar hall and knocked on Briggs's door. No answer. He touched the opening rune and glanced inside. Briggs lay sprawled on the bed, snoring softly. No surprise he was still asleep. Teleporting them both so far, even if Grimshadow and the Reaper had provided the power, must've taken a big toll.

Best let him sleep as long as he needed to. Danny closed the door and moved a little ways away.

"Riko."

She must've been waiting nearby as hardly any time passed before she came trotting up the stairs. All signs of the previous day's battle were gone. Even her dark uniform had been repaired. Since he doubted she knew how to sew, some magic had to be involved.

She bowed in greeting. "Good morning, Daniel. I trust you slept well?"

"I did. Nothing like a fight to the death to wear you out. Let's take a walk. I want to visit the library. On my travels I picked up something I think the librarian will appreciate."

"As far as I can tell," Riko said, "he appreciates nothing save books."

"Exactly."

Riko gave him a confused look, drawing a laugh from Danny. "I picked up some evil magic stuff on my way here. This seems like a safe place to store it. You guys can add it to all the other evil stuff you've got lying around."

"You know most magic isn't good or evil, right? It all comes down to how you use it."

Danny started down the steps. "The people I took it from weren't using it for good, I can assure you. Speaking of, any idea what those two wanted here?"

"Power, I assume. There are a lot of secrets hidden here. Any wizard would give just about anything for access." Riko shook her head. "If you and Briggs hadn't arrived when you did, I would be dead and Astaroth's followers would be consecrating the Reaper's temple to their master right now."

"I'm glad we got here in time then."

"As am I." Riko's face betrayed nothing, but Danny sensed the emotion behind her words. Demons weren't supposed to feel fear, but Riko had come close to being destroyed and sent back to the Reaper's hell. He couldn't blame her for being relieved.

They reached the library doors. Danny pushed them open, breathing in the scent of parchment and leather. Though far from a real scholar, he had spent a fair bit of time here trying to figure out how to destroy the ether pools, so his return felt a bit nostalgic.

Danny strode into the cavernous library and went over to the table he'd used all those weeks. It looked like nothing had changed. The rows of books were perfectly orderly with nary a mote of dust to be seen.

"Librarian," Danny said. "I brought you a present."

A dark, cowled figure emerged from the stacks and glided toward them. The librarian's empty cowl turned to focus on Danny. "You again. I can't imagine you bringing anything I might be interested in."

"We'll see." Danny opened his storage and started piling books up on the table. When all of them covered the table and floor he added a bunch of scrolls to the pile. "Not too shabby if I do say so myself. Think these would make a good addition to the library's collection?"

The librarian ran a skeletal hand over the cover of the top book like it was his long-lost lover. "Do you know, in all my years as librarian, we haven't added a single new book to the collection? This is a glorious day. Perhaps I was mistaken about your uselessness."

"Thanks." Danny figured that was as close as he was going to get to a compliment from the grouchy demon. He had no use for the books and they took up a lot of room in his storage space. They'd be safe in the library and if he ever needed them, he knew where they'd be. "I could use some fresh air. Let's take a walk."

They left the librarian fondling his gift and Danny led the way out into the city center. It was another beautiful day spoiled only by the ambient corruption of the city. His barrier of holy energy kept it from being uncomfortable.

"How are the city's defenses?" he asked.

Riko's beautiful face twisted. "We lost a quarter of our guardian demons, but they'll regenerate in a few weeks. The fight with Berend made it clear I'm not strong enough on my own to stop an enemy of his strength should another show up."

"That's not ideal. I hate the idea of this place falling into the hands of a group of less agreeable evil people and not just because I might need access to the library in the future. We're going to have to do something about your security situation."

"Like what?" Riko asked. "We'd need a source of life energy to summon reinforcements and you don't strike me as the sort to be interested in human sacrifice."

"You know me too well. Over the course of my last mission, in addition to the books I donated to your library, I acquired a large quantity of ether crystals. I was thinking they might serve as a source of replacement energy for the summoning."

"I'm not aware of such a thing ever happening," Riko said. "We should ask the master."

Danny nodded and Riko led the way through the streets back to the tower where Danny arrived. As they neared the Reaper's temple the corruption grew thicker. It would never be pleasant, but he'd at least gotten a bit used to the sickening feeling.

They entered the tower and descended to the temple. The statue of a cloaked figure, like an oversized version of the librarian, loomed over the black altar. It had a particularly strong presence today.

Riko bowed to the statue and explained Danny's idea.

An interesting suggestion. The Reaper's cold voice echoed in Danny's head. *It should work, though it will be less efficient than using life energy. Place the crystals on my altar. We shall see what can be done.*

"I will prepare the ritual," Riko said.

While she got busy with the magic, Danny opened his storage and carefully laid two-thirds of his collection of ether crystals on the altar. The rest he'd keep as a rainy-day fund. The faceted stones glittered in the temple's eerie light.

As soon as he moved out of the way, Riko cast her spell and a black disk appeared in the air above the altar. One by one, the ether crystals shattered, and the contained energy flowed into the darkness.

When the last wisp of ethereal energy vanished, three figures emerged from the disk. Their wings were black as midnight and their eyes glowed with crimson light. The demons looked like sisters to Riko. Only a few subtle differences in their face and figure separated them.

Riko smiled. "Welcome, sisters."

He thought they might embrace, but that wasn't a very demonic thing to do. Instead the new arrivals landed, wrapped their wings around their bodies, and bowed to the statue.

Leave us now. I would have a word with Daniel, alone.

No one questioned the Reaper's order and in moments he was alone in the temple.

"What's on your mind?" Danny asked.

What you have done here today will mark you as an enemy of Heaven. Do you understand that?

Danny cocked his head. "How do you figure? I just wanted to help my friend. Riko should be a lot better off with a bit of heavy-duty backup."

The Reaper's laughter sent a chill up his spine. *You summoned demons, boy. That's not the sort of thing Heaven will overlook. You might as well pledge yourself to me at this point.*

"Technically you're correct, but I didn't kill anyone to do it. That's the bit that stains your soul, right? I also didn't cast the summoning spell, Riko did. I only provided the crystals. All things considered, I think I'll be okay. Adonael is more likely to be pissed at me for destroying the ether pool."

You play with fire, boy. Be careful you don't burn yourself.

The Reaper's presence vanished and Danny sighed. How did he end up on better terms with a demon lord than an archangel? Probably best not to think about it.

He left the temple and went outside to find Riko waiting. The other black-winged angels had flown off somewhere, probably on patrol.

"Thank you, Daniel, for doing this for us. With my sisters here, the city will be safe from anything short of a full invasion."

"I'm glad I could help. I probably shouldn't be so fond of a demon, but it would sadden me if anything happened to you."

She leaned in and kissed his cheek. "Most humans can't see anything but a demon when they look at me, but I remember my life as a human. It's nice to have a real friend. When will you leave?"

"As soon as Briggs wakes up. We need to rejoin the beast-folk. Once they're sorted out, I'll head for the next ether pool. It might be a while before we see each other again."

She sighed. "I fear you're right, but I shall look forward to that day."

With a snap of her wings, Riko leapt into the air. Danny watched until she was little more than a dark spot against the blue sky then turned back to the central tower. Hopefully Briggs would be awake and ready to go.

Pleasant as this little break had been, he had a mission to complete.

CHAPTER 32

Late in the evening, after two weeks of nearly nonstop walking, Danny and Briggs spotted the beastfolk. The group had set up camp in a forest clearing far from anything resembling civilization, a precaution Danny wholly approved of. Everyone looked unharmed, and slices of meat were roasting over an open fire. The scene reassured Danny that, despite everything they'd been through, the beastfolk were still capable of managing on their own.

He'd been a bit worried about it given the deference they'd showed him. Perhaps they were just afraid. Danny hated to think so, but it wasn't beyond the realm of possibility. He'd cut down enough people in front of them after all.

Beside him Briggs let out a long sigh. "They're okay. Thank heaven."

"We're far enough from Crystal Lake that the odds of slave hunters showing up are minimal," Danny said. "Come on, let's go see everyone."

Briggs led the way. Danny sensed guards placed around

the perimeter of the camp, but they must've recognized the pair as they made no effort to challenge them. As soon as they were close, Briggs broke into a run and was soon hugging his mother. Danny smiled. Killing monsters and destroying the ether pool were all well and good, but it was nice to just see people looking happy.

When Briggs finally let go of his mother, Danny joined them. "Glad you're all doing well."

"We were worried about the two of you," she said. "How bad was the fight?"

"Bad enough, but we came through it in one piece and that's the main thing. Your group has made good progress. If you can keep up this pace, we should reach the others in a couple weeks. There is another option."

Darla cocked her head. "Such as?"

"You could keep going as you are and I'll run ahead, collect Val and the others, and meet you all halfway. I'm not sure where your territory is exactly, but there's no sense in you walking farther than you have to and then backtracking. What do you think?"

"We should join up with Val as soon as possible," Briggs said.

"It would be good to reunite with everyone and Val may have plans for our new territory, assuming he doesn't want to return to our old hunting grounds." Darla nodded. "That's fine."

Danny swallowed a sigh of relief. He had no desire to trudge along at the pace this group could manage. "As long as you keep moving due east from here, you'll have no trouble, especially with Briggs here to protect you."

"You'll at least stay the night, right?" Briggs sounded a bit nervous. Danny wasn't sure why since he'd already protected the group once on his own.

"Yes, it's too late to leave now anyway, though I plan to set out at first light. On my own I should be able to reach the outpost in three days. I wish there was an easy way to bring you with me, but I don't know any magic capable of such a feat."

Darla smiled. "Don't trouble yourself about it. We're free and together. That's more than enough for now."

Danny appreciated her attitude. Since there was nothing more to be said he drifted off to give mother and son a chance to catch up. He settled on a spot at the edge of the group under a large spruce tree.

He had great respect for the beastfolk, but he had no desire to settle down with them. The sooner he could reunite both groups, the sooner he could move on to the next ether pool.

Speaking of. He took his map out of storage. The one he'd dealt with was the closest to Elfhome. Based on its position, it was clear that the map was less accurate than he might've hoped. The pools weren't evenly spaced around the continent. Instead they appeared to be about a few thousand miles apart from each other, but the farthest out from Elfhome was over ten thousand miles away and a thousand miles inland from the coast.

Danny growled a little and put the map away for now. There had to be a reason for the seemingly random distances, but damned if he understood them. And in the end the exact distance didn't make much difference. If he got close enough, he should be able to sense the magic and home in on it.

But one mission at a time. First the beastfolk, then he'd swing by Discourt and update Mother Ankie. Once that was done, he could decide which ether pool to visit next.

○

Briggs walked with his fellow beastfolk through familiar plains that were their natural home. The air was almost warm today and he could smell the new shoots of grass poking out of the ground. The group had left the forest behind several days ago and he'd heard a couple of hunters from a different pack saying they were pretty sure this was their home range.

He'd halfway expected them to break off from the main group, but so far no one had. He figured they were all waiting until Ronin returned with the second group of former slaves.

For his part, Briggs couldn't wait to see Val again. Something about their pack leader always made him feel at ease. He was also eager to turn over the responsibility of overseeing the group to someone with more experience. Briggs had done his best, but he wasn't even an adult yet. There was no way he should be in charge.

At least he'd paid the Reaper back for giving him Grimshadow.

You never completely pay back the master. You will serve him as necessary for the rest of your life and your soul will be his when you die. You're only lying to yourself if you believe otherwise.

Briggs grimaced, but deep down knew Grimshadow was right. He was lying to himself. It was necessary to help him sleep at night. He had no idea what sort of tasks the Reaper might require of him and he didn't want to think about the possibilities.

A piercing whistle brought him up short. One of the hunters who served as an advance scout had stopped up ahead. The whistle meant someone was headed their way. Briggs ran ahead and stopped beside the hunter. He shaded his eyes and scanned the horizon. Soon enough he spotted a modest group coming right toward them. They were still too far away to make out any details, but Briggs was pretty sure they were beastfolk. Since there were too many for a single pack, that meant it had to be Ronin with Val's group.

Finally!

Briggs waved the rest of the group up. His mother and a couple of the others who had taken on a leadership role during the march came to join him beside the scout.

"Is it them?" his mother asked.

Briggs nodded. "I'm pretty sure, but we'll know without a doubt in a few minutes."

Everyone was talking at once, murmuring, hoping some missing loved one was with this group and not buried somewhere. The hard part was going to come when Val arrived and they knew for sure who survived. Some people were going to find that ones they'd been hoping to see were really gone.

Distances on the plains were deceptive and it took nearly half an hour for Ronin to lead Val and the others to them. As soon as they arrived the group broke up into hugging family groups. Briggs found Ronin standing a little ways away watching the celebration.

"You did it," Briggs said.

Ronin shook his head. "I just helped out a little. Your people did most of it themselves. How are you holding up?"

"We're all fine. Beastfolk are used to walking."

"Not what I meant." Ronin gave Grimshadow a meaningful look.

"Oh, right." Briggs told him what the demon had said. "Sounds like I'm still bound to the Reaper's service. I didn't want to admit it to myself, but I'm not surprised. It was worth any price for this moment."

Ronin made no comment which Briggs appreciated. Maybe he was lying to himself, but that was fine. He just wanted to enjoy the moment.

Once he'd finished saying his hellos, Val strode over to the pair. He held out his hand to Briggs, who shook it in the beastfolk way. "You did well. I spoke to your mother, and Ronin told me everything on our walk here. No hunter could've done more for our pack."

Briggs's cheeks warmed. He didn't know what to say about the praise, so he just nodded. "Thanks. It's good to have you back, Val."

"It's good to be back." Val turned to Ronin. "What will you do now, my friend?"

"Continue my mission. I need to make a visit to Discourt then I'm heading for the next ether pool. I wish you and your people all the best. Think on what I said."

"I will. A confederacy of packs is an intriguing idea, one I'd never considered. Good luck and know that you will always be welcome in our territory." They shook then Ronin waved and turned south toward the human city.

Briggs watched until he was out of sight. In his heart he knew he would likely never see his human friend again.

Val clapped him on the shoulder. "Come, let us join the others. There is much to discuss and you have earned your place at the fire."

Briggs wiped his eyes and followed his pack leader back to the group. He would do his best to help for as long as the Reaper allowed.

EPILOGUE

D anny strode through the familiar streets of Discourt on his way to the Temple of the Goddess. The air was almost warm, at least compared to a month ago, and people were out in force. The fear of the plague was nowhere to be seen thanks to the priests' efforts. It was a nice change and Danny very much appreciated it.

A week ago he'd reunited Val and the others held at the elf outpost with their loved ones. There had been much hugging and celebrating. Danny didn't stick around long after completing his mission. The beastfolk had important decisions to make and he had no part to play in the process. No, he'd shaken hands with everyone, gotten a standing invite to return anytime, and departed.

Hopefully they'd be okay, especially with Briggs and Grimshadow to help with security. But whatever happened, it was outside Danny's control.

He entered the temple district and made his way toward

the sprawling temple. It looked exactly as he remembered and thankfully there was no line of sick people waiting for treatment. The healers' was the one place you liked to see lacking customers.

In the entry area one of the cute priestesses was on duty behind the desk. Danny couldn't remember her name, but she looked vaguely familiar. Of course they all looked familiar with their blond hair, pale skin and white robes.

"Hello," Danny said. "My name is Ronin and I was hoping I could speak to Mother Ankie if she's available."

"Mr. Ronin, of course. I have a note here that says you're to be announced whenever you wish. I believe Mother Ankie is in the chapel. You can go right in." She motioned toward the door behind her.

Danny smiled. "Thanks. Oh, before I forget, is Michael around or did he head back to Redfield?"

"He joined the healing caravan with Sister Bernadette. He's going to ask Father Sander for a reassignment to the caravan when they reach Redfield. If his superior says yes, Michael is going to ask Bernadette to marry him." She let out a little giggle. "Isn't that exciting?"

Danny nodded. "Very. I hope it works out for them. Excuse me."

He left the priestess behind and stepped into the nearly empty chapel. Mother Ankie sat in the front pew, head bowed in prayer. Danny made a point of stepping a bit louder than strictly necessary and halfway up the aisle she raised her head and smiled at him. She looked well rested and her color was good. He was pleased to see she had fully recovered from the effects of the poison.

"Mother Ankie," Danny said.

"Ronin, what a nice surprise. I wasn't sure if I'd see you again."

"I wasn't either, but I needed to buy supplies and wanted to give you an update on the plague, so I decided to swing by Discourt. You're looking well."

"Oh, yes, I'm all better. And a good thing too since I doubt Father Koen would've left had it been otherwise." She patted the pew beside him. "Have a seat and tell me everything."

Danny settled in beside her and filled her in on all he'd learned about the plague. He left out helping to summon three demons. That could lead to a misunderstanding.

"I don't know if blessing the remains of the dead is something the priests in the caravan can do, but you might want to mention it to them, assuming you have some way to keep in touch."

"I will." Mother Ankie shook her head. "I never imagined the cult of Astaroth was involved. Though it does explain the sudden mutation of the disease. I'm relieved the priest and his followers have been dealt with."

"Likewise. I hope the area will know a bit of peace now. Heaven knows you've all earned it."

"Where will you go now?"

Danny shrugged. "Since spring is here, I'll probably head north. That will be a lot more pleasant in the summer than winter. I'll accomplish as much as I can before turning back south for the winter."

"I wish you the best of luck in your efforts."

Danny stood. "Thanks. I doubt we'll meet again and I wanted to say it's been a pleasure to make your acquaintance. Be well."

With a final bow, Danny turned and marched out. He

needed to buy supplies then it would be time to hit the road again. After studying his map, he planned to visit an area to the northeast with the disconcerting name of the Forest of Drakes.

BONUS CHAPTER - THE FIVE KINGDOMS RECOVERY PLAN PART 2

High Priestess Eve Carre carefully adjusted the altar cloth, making sure Adonael's halo symbol was centered. Tomorrow was Holy Day and she wanted everything to be perfect when the people arrived. His Majesty King Florian had been attending every week as well which was nice but different from his father who seldom came save on important holidays.

The new king had been in a poor mood since Lady Shael left the city. Eve hadn't seen or heard anything from her friend since she left. It was hard to believe Florian had been foolish enough to try and force the elf-bloods to join the army.

Then again, having met Duke Morel, it wasn't impossible to believe he'd suggest something so stupid. Alban was a buffoon with far too much influence. Something needed to be done about him before he ran Villipan completely into a ditch.

Not that Eve was the one to handle it.

As she was making the final adjustment, a tremor shook

the cathedral. Jagged lines like lightning bolts ran through the crystal walls. Eve's hair stood on end and she looked everywhere for the source of the strange magic. Nothing like that had ever happened and she'd never read anything about it either.

"What in the—"

She didn't have a chance to finish the sentence before she found herself facing Adonael amidst the clouds and white light of Heaven. Her patron didn't look pleased. Her normally serene expression was turned down in a deep frown and the very air trembled with her anger.

"Adonael?" Eve asked in a trembling voice.

The archangel made a visible effort to calm herself.

"Is all well?" Eve asked.

"No. Daniel has succeeded in destroying a small part of the summoning spell. I didn't believe him capable of it, but somehow he has done the impossible. And if he did it once, he can do it again. We may well be in danger of losing our only advantage over the demon lords."

Eve wasn't sure what to say so she remained silent.

"He has forced me to take more aggressive measures to stop him." Adonael gave a little shake of her head. "But no matter. That isn't something you need to concern yourself with. The reason I summoned you here now is a more local problem. Your new king is failing. The Five Kingdoms must be ready to face Ardent Lilly's demon king when she returns, yet he has made no progress toward rebuilding the army. You will speak to him and make my displeasure clear. Things must change if your world is to survive."

"What should I say?" Eve asked. "I know nothing about war and strategy. I only advise Florian on matters of faith and healing."

"You need not tell him how to do it, only what has to be done. You are my chosen and they will ignore your words at their peril. Tell them to focus on rebuilding the army and preparing their defenses. When the time for the next battle comes, they will face it without the hero. If the Five Kingdoms is at anything less than complete readiness, you will fail. I will attempt to maneuver Daniel into conflict with the demon king before that happens, but my ability to act directly on your world is limited. I am counting on you, my chosen."

Eve blinked and found herself back in the chapel. Her knees were weak and she sat beside the altar before she could fall. Convincing Florian to do what Adonael wanted would be no easy task and even if she succeeded, Eve wasn't confident he had the ability to carry out the task.

She sighed then smiled. But at least Daniel was still alive. Though it may not please her patron, Eve, at least, was happy to hear it. She gathered herself and stood. Best to speak with Florian as soon as possible. The longer she thought about it, the more nervous she'd get.

Heaven's mercy she wished Lady Shael was here, this would be so much easier with her help.

AUTHOR NOTE

Hello everyone,

Danny never expected to run into someone from his old world, much less in the form of a demon. But they got along well all things considered. I hope you're excited t see what happened when Danny arrives in the Forest of Drakes

If you don't want to miss any of my new releases, deals, general news about the Etherverse, you can signup for my newsletter on my website.

www.jamesewisher.com

Until next time, thanks for reading,

James E. Wisher

Malice

Hearts of Corrupt Fire

Ultima Thule

Aegis of Merlin Omnibus Vol 1.

Aegis of Merlin Omnibus Vol 2.

The Complete Aegis of Merlin Omnibus

The 72 Demons

The Blood of Solomon

A Friend in Need

The Demon Masks

Hunt For The Devil Man

The Immortal Apprentice Trilogy

The War With Audin (Prequel Novella)

The Hunt For Revenge

The Army of Darkness

The Apprentice Reborn

The Soul Bound Saga

An Unwelcome Journey

Darkness in Tiber

Depths of Betrayal

The Black Iron Empire

Overmage

The Divine Key Trilogy

Shadow Magic

For The Greater Good

The Divine Key Awakens

The Portal Wars Saga

The Hidden Tower

The Great Northern War

The Portal Thieves

The Master of Magic

The Chamber of Eternity

The Heart of Alchemy

The Sanguine Scroll

Shadow of The Dragons

The Dragonspire Chronicles

The Black Egg

The Mysterious Coin

The Dragons' Graveyard

The Slave War

The Sunken Tower

The Dragon Empress

The Dragonspire Chronicles Omnibus Vol. 1

The Dragonspire Chronicles Omnibus Vol. 2

The Complete Dragonspire Chronicles Omnibus

Soul Force Saga

Disciples of the Horned One Trilogy:

Darkness Rising

Raging Sea and Trembling Earth

Harvest of Souls

Disciples of the Horned One Omnibus

Chains of the Fallen Arc:

Dreaming in the Dark

On Blackened Wings

Chains of the Fallen Omnibus

The Complete Soul Force Saga Omnibus

Other Fantasy Novels:

The Squire

Death and Honor Omnibus

The Rogue Star Series:

Children of Darkness

Children of the Void

Children of Junk

Rogue Star Omnibus Vol. 1

Children of the Black Ship

Children of The End

ABOUT THE AUTHOR

James E. Wisher is a writer of science fiction and Fantasy novels. He's been writing since high school and reading everything he could get his hands on for as long as he can remember.

www.ingramcontent.com/pod-product-compliance
Lightning Source LLC
Chambersburg PA
CBHW030538030726
47495CB00004B/1037